The Plant That Ate The World

by the same author

The Shaman's Stone

ff

THE PLANT
THAT ATE
THE WORLD

Hugh Scott

faber and faber
LONDON · BOSTON

First published in 1989
by Faber and Faber Limited
3 Queen Square London WC1N 3AU

Photoset by Parker Typesetting Service Leicester
Printed in Great Britain by
Richard Clay Ltd Bungay Suffolk

A CIP record for this book is available from the British Library

ISBN 0-571-15440-9

for
JAMIE
with love

The island sang louder after the summer storm. Steam rose, and the smell of earth attracted the blackbird.

Rain retreated over the town, and Tomlin tilted his head letting his mouth gape as he looked straight up, and he grinned at the sky because it was blue, and at the little clouds because they were white. And the water rushed, blue and white around the island, turning to cream as it frothed against cement and rock; and Tomlin stared, not smiling, at the arms of land and big islands to the west. They were green. Green and dark, with mist curling above them. He turned again to the town on the mainland, the town that clung to the coast as if pushed towards the water by the green mass beyond.

'Tomlin!'

Grandfather's voice pitched high above the island's song.

'Hurry!'

Tomlin ran, lifting a basket from the rail around the house, along the metal path, his feet slapping down with an almost hollow noise, on to the rocks where the island met the scurrying water.

His hands flickered gathering pods, rushing them into the basket, dark green in the basket, bean pods, longer than your hand, layering deeper, drying, as water slid off.

1

Grandfather's basket filled quicker, because he had more fingers than Tomlin, but he grinned and Tomlin grinned back and tried to go twice as fast, but he only missed, making Grandfather's left eye crinkle warningly, then Grandfather laughed with all his teeth, and shook his head, not trying to speak above the island's song.

Tomlin nodded upstream, and they paused, watching where the current squeezed around the promontory, and Tomlin shook a little fist at the promontory's dark green tousled life – the Plant, wrestling with itself, thick as a man's body, tapering to pencil-thin tips higher than Grandfather's head, flowers like soft faces sunbathing; and in the current a raft of pods, floating towards their island.

'The pole!' cried Grandfather, and Tomlin leapt, and Grandfather's fingers all grasped the pole's handle, and Tomlin, gripping the middle, plunged into the water, the far end with the flat pusher advancing towards the pods;

meeting the pods; holding them –

'Forward!' cried Tomlin.

And forward they stepped, Grandfather's strength controlling the pole, Tomlin guiding, wet to the hips.

'Lean!'

They leaned, resisting the raft,

'Forward!'

heaving! and Tomlin stumbled, knees on rock, water round his throat, but holding the pole, succeeding,

'Withdraw!'

and he laughed in the water, and behind him

2

Grandfather laughed and the island sang as the pods slid into another current and went turning past the island, clinging briefly to the mast of the sunken yacht, then out of sight behind the hump of lawn, where the greenhouse sparkled with glass and splashed the eye with colour.

'Out you come!' yelled Grandfather, and he hauled the pole, and Tomlin waded ashore, peering at his knees, blood on his knees, shorts and shirt transparent with water.

He pulled his shirt off and gave it to the rocks to dry, and pick! pick! went his three fingers, making pods leap into the basket. Grandfather's basket was full and weighed as much as two Tomlins and a Sequence, but Grandfather lifted it, hooking its handle on the cruel hook that hung from the pulley. Then he went up the two steps built around the concrete post and turned the wheel, sending the basket along the rope, dangling like a dead man, water squirting where the rope met the steel pulley-wheel, so squeal! said the rope and the basket went swinging across the lawn, past the house, across the carrots and onions, through the orchard, over the pleasant green slope of potatoes, and by the time it stopped it looked no bigger than a sock on a washing line.

'Now mine!' cried Tomlin.

'Now yours!' cried Grandfather, and rope squealed, and the island sang and Tomlin's feet beat like a drum on the metal path, past the greenhouse, pattering between the carrots and onions, dodging in the orchard, racing down the long slope of potatoes.

And he got under the first dangling man and pushed up with his shoulders tipping the basket free of the hook, tipping its mouth to the south shore, spewing the pods on to a concrete chute, sending them skittering into the water; where the current curled hungrily and gobbled the pods deep, deep and away from the island, then bobbing up, rushing southwards mingling with the waves.

Then he emptied the second basket, and ran with the baskets rough on his shoulders, ran to the north shore and began again, picking, flicking the pods until the rocks and cement of the shore were clean, and they sat, Tomlin and his grandfather waiting for the great river to bring more beans.

Then the baskets, partly full, went drunkenly along the rope, the beans given back to the water, the baskets hung on the rail around the house, and the sun hammered the island with heat until there was no more steam, and Tomlin's shorts dried opaque, and the blackbird stretched a worm from the earth.

Sequence welcomed them by sticking his head through the rail, trotting along the boards of the veranda and defending the steps as Tomlin and Grandfather ascended to the house.

'Lazy mutt!' said Grandfather. 'You ought to brush that dog. I remember sheep less woolly than him. Why weren't you helping?' he growled as Sequence wagged a tail no thicker than Grandfather's whip. 'And I remember when little square dogs had little square tails.

Snip, snip at the vet, you old rogue, or before vets, bitten off by m'teeth!'

'Grandfather!' gasped Tomlin.

And Grandfather laughed, displaying his teeth to the sun, ruffling Tomlin's hair, ruffling Sequence, assuring Tomlin that he'd never chewed anything tougher than new thongs for his whip.

In the kitchen Grandfather shook the gas tank, lit the cooker above the tank, found a cigar in the cupboard at his face and relaxed in his armchair at the north window. 'Aren'tchy'going to make the coffee? Y've seen me before.'

Tomlin blinked and turned to the kettle, opened the five-hundred gram tin of coffee –

'You didn't really bite a dog's tail, Grandfather?'

Grandfather bellowed with laughter, but he still faced the north window of this long narrow room. 'Never!' he roared. 'Perhaps,' he said, 'when my father was a boy, *some* people did. To save a shilling or two.'

Tomlin put coffee and sugar into mugs, and sat on a foam-soft seat, watching the kettle's spout. 'Were there lots of dogs?'

'Lots,' growled Grandfather.

'And this wasn't a real house?'

'No.'

'A caravan.'

'A caravan. And another. And another. Side-by-side, until I'd a square place to live in. Bolted them together with these ten fingers. Cut doors where I had to. Three toilets. Three showers. Three kitchens. Room for you and your mother and me . . .'

5

'And all metal and plastic.'

'Aye. Metal and plastic. Indigestible metal and plastic. And this island.'

The kettle wheezed. Tomlin poured, gritting his teeth at the steam. Took the coffees to the north window. Leaned back in the bench seat, holding the three fingers of his left hand as if they nursed a cigar, gripped the mug with his right hand but couldn't quite lift it, so he laid his cigar carefully on the edge of the table the smoking end in empty air and used both hands to raise the mug. Sip. Puff away steam. Sip.

Sequence clicked with claws in the kitchen, looked at Tomlin, at Grandfather, sighed through his nose, and went out.

'What makes the island sing, Grandfather?' He knew what made the island sing, but coffee time – especially coffee time after the rain when the bean pods fall – was story time; time to know, to remember; time, hopefully, to learn of past errors and to scream to Heaven if anyone should contemplate the errors again.

'We built things, my father and me. Houses, schools, blocks of flats – '

'The red-brick flats – '

'The red-brick flats beyond the church, where the Poor Souls skulk in darkness because they don't know how to light a fire or connect a gas cylinder . . .'

'They'd be better off in an old house with a fireplace where they could burn the mountain of coal in the depot behind the station, or learn how to dry the Plant and use it for fuel – '

'Hmm!' said Grandfather. 'Who's telling this story?'

' Go on, Grandfather!'

'Anyway. I knew a thing or two about driving machinery, and after the war, oh, so long after! when the mutant runner bean was discovered – !'

Tomlin watched for Grandfather's snarl, and Grandfather snarled around his cigar. 'They experimented. An endless food source with few left to eat it – '

'The submarines,' urged Tomlin.

'It thrived on poisoned ground. Then they couldn't stop it. But it was seeded in every continent. Perhaps we shouldn't blame them too much. It was good to eat at first. But in the third season, the flavour was bland, and the soil was recovering anyway; agriculture creeping back.

'By the fourth year the Plant was inedible, and no amount of weedkiller could – '

Grandfather took a long gulp of coffee. Tomlin went to Grandfather's bedroom in the next caravan. The tantalus was dusty. Tomlin carried it, using both little fists to grip the handle, into the kitchen, where he used a duster to bring up the shine of the silver hinges, the silver lock; to burnish the grain of the oak. Then he placed it at Grandfather's hand on the chair arm, and Grandfather said 'Hmm!' and crinkled his eye at Tomlin, but he held the box and balanced his cigar on the table the smoking end in empty air; stroked the box, all his fingers loving the hard smooth feel of the wood, then he clicked the lock and hoisted from within, one of the three crystal decanters and a matching glass from its velvet nest, and poured *just that* much brandy. He placed the tantalus on the floor,

7

raised the glass to Tomlin, and sipped.

'The submarine,' said Tomlin.

'Well,' sighed Grandfather. 'You know how clever your old Grandad is. I saw what was coming. So I thought it out – '

'Because you were clever.'

'I thought it out. The Plant was unstoppable. I had to find a place for us where the Plant couldn't grow – or if it did – '

'You could pull it up!'

Grandfather sipped. The crystal glass sparkled colours in the sunlight. Tomlin looked out at the promontory and the high arm of land beyond. Dark green and curling like hair, the blue water shimmering, protecting the island.

'Wherever it grew, down went roots so deep and fine – Well, I thought, shallow soil with no rock underneath for roots to penetrate – But what a problem! Where? I asked myself! Where is soil without rock!'

'One day – '

'Then one day – ' Grandfather's grey eyebrows rose dangerously, ' – I was exploring the old submarine base. They'd been lying for donkey's years, and I went clumping around, clang! clang! wondering what the scrap value would've been! Haw! Haw! Haw! Haw! Scrap value,' sighed Grandfather. 'There wasn't a pound in circulation. Banks were heaped with money. Not a soul bothered. Except a few, maybe, who'd lost sight of reality. Oh. Oh, well. Where was I?'

'The submarines.'

'Fetch your Grandad some more coffee.'

8

'Oh, Grandfather!'

'Go on, go on, go on! I'll shout it to you.'

'Ooh!' said Tomlin, and ran to the kitchen with Grandfather's mug and rattled around the coffee tin with a spoon.

'And there I was,' said Grandfather, his voice pitched high to cover the distance, to rise above the song of the island. 'Just for fun, thinking how I could tow a submarine down the loch – not that I had any use for a submarine! But it was fun solving the problem, and then –'

Tomlin hurried back with the coffee. He snuggled into the seat. 'Then? Then!'

'Then I saw it.' Grandfather gazed past Tomlin, glass sparkling in the sunlight, cigar smoke streaming. 'Then – I – saw – it! There! Just there! Between the submarine and the dock; over the years, winter and summer, spring and autumn, day and night, hour by hour –'

Tomlin squirmed.

'Earth had gathered. Earth, Tomlin, and in the earth, a little tree. A little tree, Tomlin, with neat oval leaflets, and berries as red as your mother's lips. And growing around it – why, grass of course! And wild flowers! And, oh, Tomlin, it began to rain.' Grandfather's eyes looked into the past. 'A drop quivering a leaf, washing the bark making the bark shine silver – like the hinges of the tantalus – and the rain darkened the soil, and Tomlin, I crouched by that tree and watched the water drip from its leaflets, trickle on the silver; and little bright jewels of liquid danced on the grass, making the flowers bend their faces . . .'

'And you shook your fist,' whispered Tomlin.

'Aye. I shook my fist at the Plant on the hills around the loch! That was as close as it had come in those days.'

Grandfather sat still, the brandy flat in the tilted glass, the eye of the cigar glowing, but the glow creeping about the tobacco as bits blackened, smoked and glowed again. 'I miss your mother,' said Grandfather.

'And Grandmother.'

Grandfather touched the cigar to his lips. 'She went quickly, thank God! Not like some poor wretches. Lingering still, some of them, I expect.'

Grandfather gulped brandy. His hair, white and thick, hung wearily.

'The story.'

'The story. Well, I had more or less worked out how to move the submarines. There was enough machinery still functioning, and a removal van I'd found behind a furniture store. So I packed in some Poor Souls, told 'em what to do, and they did it. Slowly. Badly. Eventually, though, with my cleverness and their hands, we did it. It wasn't as difficult as I'd feared, mind you. I had to do all the welding myself. That was hard. And we filled steel drums with concrete, the ends of great chains pushed in deep, and used them for anchors. Chains as thick as your leg taking the strain of sixteen metal sardines! That's what they were like! Sardines! This way and that! Packed tight, welded hard. Sixteen submarines and half a dredger! That's what's under our feet! That's what keeps us afloat! And chains thick as your leg – have I said that? Anchoring it. I had to be clever then. I measured the tide. Right here I gauged the water at high tide. The highest tide in the almanack! Then I added a bit for good luck – in case of floods. And that was the length of my chains.

'It took an army of Poor Souls to move these chains. Poor Souls.'

'The soil.'

'Huh,' sighed Grandfather. His head went back against the armchair and he sucked a red eye on to the cigar. He breathed smoke, and Tomlin watched the smoke twisting into layers in the sunlight. He rose and took the cigar from Grandfather's five-fingered hand, stole a little suck, then put it into the glass ashtray which Grandfather only used to crush the butt.

'I'll check the lines,' murmured Tomlin to the sleeping face.

'Mm,' said the face, and Tomlin went on to the veranda where Sequence wiggled an eyebrow at him, but otherwise sprawled with his stomach towards the sun, limp as a dead salmon. And Tomlin strode among the carrots and onions, smiled at the green bundles of plums in the orchard, down the slope of potatoes. To the little shore of rock and cement that Grandfather had built to keep the soil on the island. And Tomlin peered along the shore, to either side of the pulley pole and chute, seeing the fishing rods secure in clefts of rock, curving to the tug of the current. Two lines stretched tight as wire. As Tomlin watched, one slackened and the rod straightened upwards, froth boiling on the water, flash! in the sunlight, coloured scales of a mullet, then the other line ran to one side, a tail flicked the air

11

and the line vibrated thin as a spider's web in the bright blue day, and for a moment, a rainbow hung in the spray.

Tomlin ran. He reeled carefully, keeping the line taut, winding quickly as the fish rushed towards him; unwinding reluctantly as the mullet barged downstream threatening the line's strength; but the battle was Tomlin's as the distance between the boiling patch of water and the island shortened; then Tomlin used the net (the loop screwed to its handle by Grandfather snug around the back of his upper arm – it will take a shark to pull that from your grasp!), dipped the net below the fish, sweeping it up the bank, a living curve glittering, dumped down well away from the water, thud! on the head with a stone; and Tomlin watched red juice seep among the fish's scales.

Then he hauled in a second mullet; and flounders from rods which bobbed bright floats above the sand-bank; and with his catch dripping in the net, and the net over his shoulder, he marched to the house.

He rested the fish in the sink and walked the length of the narrow room. Grandfather's head had slipped stopping on his shoulder; hair thick as a wig, one eye staring bluely at the floor, the other shut, asleep, his shirt with grey hair peeping from between buttons, moving as he breathed, snoring in his nose.

'Grandfather.' Tomlin shook his knee gently, and the open eye moved, then woke up, and Grandfather grinned with his teeth and stretched, tendons clicking in his elbows.

'We've got two mullet and some flounders,' said Tomlin.

'The flounders'll get us a tin of coffee. Put the flag up, boy. Anything else we need?'

'Matches.'

'You know what to do. Off you go.'

Tomlin took the crystal glass with him. He washed it carefully over the fish, turning off the tap quickly, for even if the tank was full after the rain, it might be long enough before blue turned grey again. He dried the glass and his hands, sniffed to be certain the smell of fish wasn't on the crystal, then returned it to the tantalus, snapped the box shut bump! Click the lock, run on little feet to Grandfather's bedroom. Shut it away. Close it in its cupboard.

Save it.

Tomlin knew to save it. There was no brandy left in the town. No whisky – which Grandfather liked less, but he liked it. And it cleaned cuts. How much coffee was in town? Tomlin remembered the flag. He ran. Past Grandfather scraping in the sink, to a cupboard taller than Tomlin; shelved, with shelves full of folded cloth of different colours. His eye stuck on the brown fold and he pulled; he found the red fold and took it. He frowned. Was there anything else? He sighed. He knew what would happen soon. But an excited shiver touched his bare back and he half hoped he would be permitted to go. He –

'Have y'fallen asleep?' came Grandfather's voice. 'Dozing in the armchair, eh! Smoking my cigars!' Tomlin snatched the flags and ran, Grandfather's laughter bellowing after him; on to the lawn; between the cables that strained to pull the flagpole in every direction; and his fingers danced on the knot, chugging the rope, sliding the two flags on to the rope, hoisting, hand-over-hand, brown and red cloth jerking limply – How does Grandfather get them to rise smoothly! – stirring in a breath of summer air.

'I hope they notice!' said Tomlin to the blackbird. 'I hope the Poor Souls notice.' He peered up the pole, screwing his eyes against the bright day, the pole peeling its white paint, the brown and red drooping now as if already tired of the heat. It had taken the Poor Souls three days once to notice their signal for salt, and the fish stank by then.

Something clanged on the veranda, and Tomlin ran, lifted the bucket of fish scales and guts dumped by Grandfather, took it to the chute, reeled in the fishing rods one by one, capturing three small flounders and a sole; he smiled at the sole; Grandfather and he would share that tonight; checked the bait, used the wicked knife in the bucket to cut meat from the fish tails, push! the hook in, hiding the hook in the bait, casting with smaller rods, letting the current take the lines out with the heavier ones.

Grandfather came through the orchard. Sequence trotting. Tomlin tipped the bucket, guts sliding down concrete, licked away by the river's wet lips.

They sat in a row, Tomlin, Grandfather, Sequence. A line straightened, and Grandfather fought a dog-fish, and up the bank it came, wriggling on its belly like a rather flat shark; but smaller. In a minute the knife had opened it, emptied its innards back to the water and Sequence ate the rest raw, coughed up bones.

14

They caught little more in the beating heat, and Tomlin was glad when they reeled in every line and Grandfather went to the house and returned balanced between two buckets of water; half full. Lay a fishing rod across one; pour water from the other, clean water, over the rod, washing salt from the reel; each reel; rods in the rock, but resting, hooks tucked away.

'I think,' shouted Grandfather, 'we deserve our lunch!' and something lurched in the sky; Tomlin clutched Grandfather's sleeve and made Grandfather face where he seldom glanced – towards the islands far away in the estuary, curling green; the lurching thing flapped steadily towards them; closer; and Grandfather's shout died to an astonished growl; motionless he waited as the thing dipped a wing and dropped to the blue surface, then rose, hovering almost, as the surface rippled suddenly with fish, and the bird swooped clattering its wings on the water, gulping, rising again, white and grey, cartwheeling in the sunlight, feathers fanning to press the air to swoop again and strike the surface, almost standing on the air –

Close.

Grandfather's hand flicked fingers towards Tomlin. His gaze stayed fastened as if by nylon line to the acrobating bird.

'The knife, boy, the knife!'

Tomlin put the plastic handle into Grandfather's grasp, then the old man crouched, glanced down for the bucket now containing fish, felt for a fish, dropped it on the earth, sliced it through –

'Grandfather – '

'Shush!'

Slice! Slice! said the knife.

'But Grandfather – '

'Be quiet! He's coming!' And Grandfather jerked his hand sending a steaklet rising against the sky. Splash! And the bird flapped closer.

Splash again.

Sinking, saw Tomlin, into a smooth patch, and the bird swept down black-tipped wings using the air, yellow bill scooping deep, gulp! Slice! went Grandfather's knife and Tomlin sighed at the diminishing sole. The bird caught the next steaklet in mid-air, then settled in the water tucking its wings back, paddling with pink feet, tilting his head to regard Grandfather with one eye.

'Oh!' said Grandfather. Tomlin threw another piece of his meal which the bird paddled after and caught.

Grandfather sat on the earth. He said 'Oh!' again, and Tomlin waited. The old man gazed as if he would suck the bird into his head.

'Oh, Tomlin!' whispered Grandfather. 'Would you believe it? D'y'know what that is? Something you've only seen in books! Is the world coming alive again! There hasn't been a seagull in the estuary since the war! What does it mean! Does it mean anything? Nothing? Tomlin! Is there hope of life again on this poor Earth! Tomlin! Tomlin! Blackbirds and starlings! And precious few of them! Did you not tell me you saw a robin in the spring and I wouldn't believe you! Is the green monster retreating? Or is this just a freak? Perhaps an island further into the Atlantic is still uncontaminated, and this creature is just silly and lost. Maybe it means nothing.'

Grandfather sat, scowling, the gull, bobbing in the water.

'I did see a robin,' breathed Tomlin.

'Aye.' Grandfather rose. 'We mustn't get our hopes up. Come on. Did you say we'd caught a sole?'

Tomlin pointed at the gull. Grandfather looked, then looked at the scraps on the earth. 'He's welcome to it.'

He led Tomlin and the dog towards the house, but his step was thoughtful and the buckets creaked forgotten in his ten fingers.

They ate potatoes from last year's crop, stored in the darkness of a garden shed; tinned peas from a shop put colour beside the fish.

Grandfather's fork clattered on the table. 'I suppose one of us will have to wash the dishes!' He burped, and Tomlin crinkled a warning eye. 'Sorry. Excuse *me*! *I* will wash up. Check the shore again, there's a good lad. Yell if you fall in.'

As Grandfather gathered the dishes, Tomlin stood close. The five-fingered hand enclosed his shoulder. 'It gets lonely,' said Grandfather.

Silence in Tomlin's head. He felt the island tilt slightly and noticed the song quieter now, as familiar as the river or the rattle of rigging on the flagpole.

'I love you, Grandfather,' he said, then he walked out of the house and invited Sequence to follow.

He started under the bridge, crawling on the shore;

17

the bridge's wheels sat rusty, but thickly greasy in the middle where they turned on the axle when the tide caused the island to rise or fall, and the bridge to roll inland or outland; and a great chain rose from the water like the skeleton of a sea monster, and the chain's end went through a loop of metal hammered deep into Grandfather's ground, and a steel wedge driven among the links, secured the chain in the loop.

Tomlin found no pods; Sequence looked, eyebrows twitching, standing still on his woolly legs, trotting suddenly to peer towards the water. He said 'Wuff,' once or twice as a wave slapped, but they found only jellyfish and drifting leaves.

Tomlin sprawled on the lawn letting the sun lean on his skin with hot fingers. He felt the island tilt and smelt the salt water of the estuary; a twist of air brought perfume, and Tomlin rolled his head looking at the startling yellows and pinks of azaleas crouching by the house, and he turned over letting the sun scratch his back. He loved the greenhouse with its special atmosphere of sweet mulch and moist heat, and honey bees yellow-legged with pollen, bouncing on glass; and he would let a bee walk on his fingers and carry it to an open part of the roof and cast it away as someone in a book might cast a hawk; but a tiny hawk, Tomlin's, bumbling heavily towards the bridge, and the hives fifty paces away on the mainland.

'Wuff!' said Sequence.

Tomlin sat up.

Two people stood beyond the bridge.

'Grandfather!' yelled Tomlin.

Grandfather came from the house pushing a floor brush, sparking the sweepings on to the veranda, resting the brush to imprison the sweepings. He disappeared then reappeared with the bucket. As he approached, Tomlin was glad that Grandfather was the biggest person in the world. The Poor Souls were tame enough, but they smiled or wept without reason.

'Come and talk to our friends,' said Grandfather, and Tomlin followed with Sequence, marching on the bridge, bare feet on warm wood, claws ticking, Grandfather striding in his deck shoes, silently. On to a lawn trimmed by Grandfather, beehives in a row, bees cutting the air into jigsaw shapes; and the Poor Souls, standing.

'They're not even waiting,' growled Grandfather, his voice rustling with anger. 'One minute is no different from the next, no, nor one year from the next. The only thing that moves them is food. Or the opposite. Or someone commanding them. This is what fear and greed have reduced us to! Thank you! Thank you!' cried Grandfather. 'Nancy! Isn't that a perfect tin of coffee!'

The Poor Soul called Nancy didn't move, but her eyes followed a bee for a moment, then stared at nothing. Sweat oozed beneath her black hair and her legs went into socks and thick shoes, legs as shapeless as Grandfather's thumbs.

'And Car! You brought matches, Car?' And Car nodded, grinning, his upper lip squashing against his nostrils, and he held out a single box of matches. 'Margrit will want a whole fish for that, eh?' and Car continued nodding. He pointed, his three fingers sweeping near

Tomlin's cheek, over Tomlin's head, at the greenhouse.

'A pot plant!' said Grandfather. 'Something bright, eh! What did she do, throw a geranium at you? Spoiled one, eh?'

Nodding.

'Come on, then. Are you coming, Nancy? Into the greenhouse? See the flowers?' Grandfather touched her arm and she paced on to the bridge, clumping, clutching the coffee.

Tomlin looked beyond the beehives on Grandfather's fresh green grass, to the broad length of weeds that stretched northwards behind the promontory, south between a church and tall buildings; a road, said Grandfather, black as your hair, a surface for tyres carrying traffic, and pavements carrying people, children. Tomlin tried to imagine it, but he could not escape what his eyes saw; weeds with a monument fingering the sky; weeds with trees softening the road and pavements, blocking shop doorways, springing from shop windows where glass hung like broken teeth. Trees and more weeds edging roofs, flowering in chimneys, solid weeds on piles of rubble. He'd found a bone once, Tomlin, picked it up thinking it was a ball, but dropped it hurriedly on turning it, finding a face more expressive than Nancy's, full of terror and sadness. Like the empty windows that stared across the estuary.

He faced the island with its neat lawn swelling over the submarines between the house and greenhouse; the controlled rows of vegetables, the luxury of colourful shrubs; the soaring flagpole with its brown signal for coffee and red for matches; and all contained within a shore of rock and cement; this was what was left, said Grandfather, of civilization.

The Poor Souls appeared from the greenhouse, Grandfather gently ushering Car towards the bridge, taking the box of matches, coaxing Nancy to release the coffee, patting her thick hand which clung to the pot plant, attracting her attention to the burst of scarlet, living petals, the geranium.

They advanced on Tomlin. Over the bridge. Car grinning closer, his upper lip wet from his nostrils, tapping Tomlin with three fingers, on his shoulder; a farewell. Tomlin tried to smile, and reminded Car to take the bucket which waited on the grass. Nancy stumped on, her face in the geranium; and they went to the road of weeds and in the centre of the road of weeds walked south; obeying Margrit's orders; too close to the buildings is bad; too close to the water is bad; so they walked safely even though the earth didn't tremble to drop stones or chimneys, even though the wind didn't blow to heave waves that might snatch them away.

'Tomlin!' called Grandfather.

Tomlin ran, Sequence clicking reluctantly behind.

'We have an invitation,' groaned Grandfather.

'Oh.'

He handed Tomlin a piece of white card. The card had rounded corners, was creased where it had been folded to go into the matchbox – 'She took most of the matches out to get that in,' sighed Grandfather. A thumb-print of green mould stained the silver writing. Margrit Bolliter (in pencil) *requests the pleasure of your company at the wedding of their daughter . . . to . . .*

21

on . . . at . . . and afterwards at . . . RSVP.

'Do we have to go?'

Grandfather drew in a slow breath, gazing at his island, the water, the hot sky. 'Yes.'

'We'll have to invite her back?'

'We must be sociable.'

'But there are so many! And only two of us! They eat so much! It's not fair – '

'Stop,' said Grandfather. 'Fair,' he said loudly, and his voice brushed the glass of the greenhouse, slipped across the water; and Grandfather's face was severe and sad. He looked down on Tomlin, took his hand, walked him round the greenhouse to the west shore where a dyke protected the greenhouse from glass-breaking waves. They sat on the dyke.

The sun chewed Tomlin's shoulders. Green mush, dark and sticky, turned against the shore then spun off in the current. Water made a necklace around the mast of the sunken yacht. The arm of land and far-off islands sat still and curling, soft mist whitening the air above them.

'Fair,' said Grandfather again.

The island sang quietly with the rush of the river on its metal body, with the hollow bong of air hauled under by water, searching the dead underside for a way to rise again.

'We seem to be born,' growled Grandfather, 'with a sense of fairness. It stays with us. It gave us the Law. You know what the Law is, boy?'

Tomlin shook his head. There were many questions like that in Grandfather's speeches. Tomlin always shook his head. 'If someone,' whispered Grandfather, 'outraged our sense of fairness, we would want to hurt him. Which was not fair.' His five fingers gripped the back of Tomlin's neck and rocked him. 'Our sense of fairness – ' he bellowed at the islands. Then he stopped. His palm patted Tomlin's shoulder, then Grandfather was searching his shirt pocket. He clicked open a cigar tin and used a match from the box brought by Car. He sucked smoke, and spoke as he breathed it out. 'We must rise above our sense of fairness. We must take fairness a step further. We must turn it into unselfishness! Not worry if someone has more than us! There is always someone, though, who will take and take until we have to say "Enough!" and now the world has died beneath the Plant – ' He threw the match on to a raft of passing mush, ' – and that's the price of greed.'

They sat, Tomlin and Grandfather, facing the water, watching the match, straight and pale, its burnt end invisible on the receding greenery. 'We'd better go. Maybe we can steal the matches she owes us.' He smiled, and Tomlin nodded up, and took his hand. 'Clean shirt,' said Grandfather.

'You too,' squeaked Tomlin.

'Something on your feet. And socks. The weeds are sharp.'

'It's a long walk for Sequence.'

'Do him good. Lazy old dog.'

They returned to the caravan, then came into the sun again, hair combed, shirts clean, Tomlin, the pressure of long socks on his legs, the weight of canvas shoes on his feet.

They crossed the bridge and solemnly said goodbye to the bees, telling them they were visiting Margrit Bolliter and would return before dark, bidding them guard the island; though who could possibly trespass neither Tomlin nor Grandfather knew.

They followed the crushed trail through the weeds where the Poor Souls had trod, between trees which were weeds. And the buildings hung above them, the sky rising blue behind scorched stone, and wild flowers stiff with heat; and the river raced, a blue sparkle, spreading to the horizon.

Grandfather led, but stopped at every avenue of weeds and trees that invited them between ruined houses, away from the river.

'Can you imagine thirty-thousand people, boy?' whispered Grandfather.

They walked between the church and high buildings, buildings full of shadow and emptiness it seemed, but the shadows glinted with ruined shop counters or furniture; or daylight poured through rafters, over crumbled heaps of brick and glass. And everywhere, signs of ancient fires. The furniture remaining was metal – wood and fabric now ash that cowered at every breeze or had long since disintegrated. And the reason there were no people, Tomlin knew, was that they too had disintegrated.

Not everyone had died. Not every shop had lost its contents. One bookshop even, tucked in a huddle of buildings, retained its window. The toy shop on a corner, partly exposed to blast, had half disappeared, leaving the other half with jigsaws on the shelves, and a row of dolls sleeping on their backs, their heads gone, the stumps of necks melted.

On the church by the shore, the steeple was charred wood, the nails holding slates liquidized by the distant bomb. Slates packed the church ground, lying thick, giant cards shuffled by an insane dealer. Pale trees leaned from pointed windows pleading for release. Tomlin shivered in the church's shadow and was relieved to see Margrit Bolliter's palace.

Rhododendrons as tall as a house, pink and scarlet, leaves like green hands, solid around the red-brick flats; glass glinting, whole in the windowframes, blue with the sky. The roof partly sunken, sycamores proud among the tiles, and a flagpole protruding below a window near the water, with a Union Jack crushed close to the red bricks, not on display. Tomlin knew that Grandfather had fastened the flagpole there, and the Union Jack would only slide out to the signalling end if someone were dying or danger threatened; that is, if the Poor Souls remembered to use it; that is, if they remembered how to use it.

Between rhododendrons they walked, Sequence peering into the tangled branches. Tomlin enjoying the mass of colour, the movement of birds.

Flies buzzing in the doorway; in the cooler hall; bin bags stacked, open, and a smell thick enough to cut with Grandfather's whip. They closed their lips tight and trotted up the stairs; Sequence pausing, nose exploring; more bags on the stairs, flies to wave away, Sequence running with sudden energy to the landing above, waiting until Tomlin opened the door, shutting

the door on the flies. Grandfather breathing out fiercely, thinly, Tomlin wanting to spit, but the floor was
clean polished lino and a carpet path that led this way
and that in wide corridors, into a broad space with large
windows giving a view of the estuary and another stair-
case; but they knew no one lived upstairs; or down.

Doors with names in little frames of brass, the names
shakily marked in pencil. Drum, read Tomlin. Nancy.
Renton. Car. Pick. Rem. Marjory. One door was
painted gold. 'Painted with a spray!' whispered Grandfather, and Tomlin saw gold faintly on the wall where
the spray had wandered, and amid the gold, red, which
was the colour Tomlin remembered from last time. The
name on this door was larger than the others, drawn on
a page from a maths jotter and using the squares on the
page to construct the letters. Margrit Bolliter. The door-
mat was new, with WELCOME woven into it, but upside-
down to the visitors; and a brass knocker awaited their
attention. Grandfather took a breath, raised his eyebrows at Tomlin, pointed a finger at Sequence, who sat;
and knocked.

A voice, shouting. Shuffling. Nancy pulling the door
open, gazing at nothing. In they went, Grandfather
crowding the little hall. Sequence avoiding legs.

'Shut the door!' cut at Nancy from a room Tomlin
could see into, sunlight filling windows, furniture shimmering with polish. 'Come through!' They went. Chair
legs and table legs glimmering, chair backs and table
tops rubbed richly brilliant. Clocks, their hands pointing stupidly, stupidly silent; ornaments from brass to
glass; pretty plates. Ugly souvenirs. Pot plants erupting

with colours, cigarette smoke in the sunlight, paintings all over the walls, hanging from the ceiling making Grandfather move his head around them. The smell of polish and sweat.

Margrit Bolliter.

An armchair filled with Margrit Bolliter.

Margrit Bolliter in a polka-dot dress, pink fingers difficult to count for the sparkle of diamonds; and feet, neat in new shoes, and her head small on her sack-of-flour neck, hair glittering black in the sun; and her eyes moved behind two pairs of spectacles, which Tomlin thought laughable, but the eyes swivelling on him were like eyes in a dead fish, and the overlapping spectacles with four legs vanishing under her hair, made him shiver.

'Well, Tomlin! See! I remember your name! That's because I'm clever!'

Tomlin opened his mouth.

'Call me Aunt Bolliter! They all do! All my friends! Only your Grandfather calls me Margrit! He's my favourite! We will have tea!' Her hand shook, and a bell in her palm jingled.

A white-haired man brought a tray with cups and saucers, plates of cakes and a silver teapot, with sugar and cream. He placed the tray on a low table. His face was young and his upper lip twitched. Tomlin stared at the tray and slid a glance at Grandfather, but he was talking and didn't seem to notice that the silver sugar bowl and the cream jug were empty.

Margrit Bolliter tipped the teapot briefly over each cup, but the teapot poured nothing and clanged with a hollow clang back on to the tray. 'Help yourself!'

Grandfather lifted a cup on its saucer, and Tomlin copied him. 'Offer my guests a cake, Rem!' And the white-haired man pushed the plate across the table.

The cake was heavy. Its yellow icing was cold and smooth on Tomlin's fingertips. It clinked as he put it on the plate.

'You like cake, Tomlin!'

'Yes – '

'That's my favourite! You like cake Markham?' she asked Grandfather.

'It's my favourite,' said Grandfather, 'but you don't fool me, Margrit – '

'Oh, I'm clever!'

'You only left ten matches in that box. You owe me matches.'

'You're having tea with me! Tea with me!' Her head quivered, sending the fat on her neck swinging, and the fish eyes burned cold.

'You're an old rascal, Margrit,' said Grandfather cheerfully. 'I comb my hair. Put on a clean shirt. Put the boy in a clean shirt. Always think I'll get round you. But I haven't yet, eh?'

'I'm clever!' said Margrit, and her head nodded suddenly, changing the rhythm of the swinging fat. 'And because you're my favourite, you can have matches. Matches! Ha! Ha!' She slid open a drawer in a desk by her chair and threw a box of matches to Grandfather. 'You missed! Ha! Ha! You never could catch! I remember! Ha! Ha! Ha! Catch these! Ha! Ha! And these! Ho! Ho! Ho! Ho! Ho!' And Grandfather continued fumbling, and grinning with embarrassment, as more boxes hit him on the forehead and shoulder, so he stumbled to his knees, and it seemed to Tomlin that Grandfather was very nimble at tucking the boxes into his trouser pockets, and when his pockets were full, passing matches to Tomlin as he knelt blocking Margrit's view.

And the woman laughed behind her two pairs of glasses, sweat on her cheeks, her black hair tilted showing bare scalp above one ear. 'Oh, yes, I'm clever!' she panted. 'No one can out-do Aunt Bolliter. But you're my favourite. Ho! Food. That's the thing, Markham! There's so much food in the town. The big shop. I won't say where it is – ' And she grinned slyly showing a row of little teeth, white, with spaces between each one. 'Ho! The food. So much! So much. There are lots of matches, though, and gas, I don't know how it survived – '

'You told me it was at the far end of town from the blast. Near the coal ree.* With rock to protect it. You remember – '

'I remember! I remember! I told you! But the food. We've eaten a lot. It'll be gone. Soon.'

'Coffee?' said Grandfather.

The head nodded swaying from side to side. 'Well . . . Enough for a year. A year. Oh I know a year!' Her fish eyes found Tomlin. 'I know a year! Warm and cold and warm again. And Christmas! My mother told me about Christmas. But I had to kill her. Ho! That's my funny! Ho! I wouldn't kill! Rem! Rem! Closer!'

* An enclosed yard for storing coal.

And she struck Rem's arm with a diamond fist and he staggered, hitting his head on a painting, making it swing, pain bringing light to his face, then he wept and Tomlin stared in horror. He saw Grandfather's fingers move on his chair and his eye crinkled, but he said nothing, though it seemed he breathed faster in his clean shirt.

'That's right,' said Grandfather quietly. 'We kill no one. There are few people left, Margrit. We need them all.'

'I know that! I know that. There's no food left.'

'Plenty of fish.'

'I have to tell them how to cook it! How to cook it! Every day! How to cook it! Tins! Tins! Tins! Tins are gone!' She struggled in the chair, the bell clucking in her palm.

'Thank you for the tea and cakes.' Grandfather rose and glanced at Tomlin.

'Thank you for the tea and cakes,' whispered Tomlin.

'You will know what to do about tins,' said Grandfather, and the creature ceased struggling and its eyes found him, and fastened on to him within its spectacle frames. 'You'll give me some of your friends and we'll go north to where there are no people, but still shops. And we'll bring back tins. Lots of tins. Eh?' And Grandfather grinned, but his eyes were without humour.

'Yes. Yes. Yes! You will go north. With my friends and . . . Ho! I'm clever. Ho!'

'Thank you for the tea. Give me a day or two, then send your friends to me. Yes? And we will bring tins. Yes?'

'Yes! Yes!'

'Get out,' muttered Grandfather, and Tomlin took Sequence.

'Yes! Yes! Yes! Yes! Yes! Yes – !'

They hurried down the stairs, through the stench and flies, into the afternoon sunlight, and the rhododendrons held flowers in green palms.

They walked without speaking. Tomlin paused to pull up his socks before entering the weeds. They walked the way they had come, north along the shore road, past the church with its pleading trees, into sunlight by the river and the monument.

'The putting green used to be there,' said Grandfather. 'There's hardly a lamppost left standing.'

The ruined town watched them pass.

'Grandfather?'

'Mm.'

'Didn't you want to hit her?'

'Yes.'

'You didn't.'

'No.'

'I wanted to kill her. She said she killed her mother.'

'I know.'

'She didn't give us anything to eat.'

Grandfather stopped. Sequence sat, panting.

'We can't always do what we feel like doing.' His hair was losing its combed look.

'But – '

'But what?'

'I'm not sure.'

'You know how to use a spade,' said Grandfather sternly.

Tomlin nodded.

'In my business we had spades that could lift a caravan. Driven by engines. Pneumatic arms. You know that.'

'Yes – '

'It was a tool for me to use.'

'Yes – '

'What if I'd left the engine running and let the spade do what it wanted? Well?'

'It . . .'

'It would have blundered about destroying everything around it.'

'Mm.'

'Without my control.'

Tomlin nodded.

'Your emotions are like that spade.' Grandfather walked on, crossing to the beehives on the lawn, assuring the bees he had returned safely with Tomlin and Sequence, and thanked them for guarding the island; and the bees sang as the island sang, but a higher song, and the sweet scent of honey clung to the air.

Then they padded over the bridge and into the house. They emptied their clothing of matches and stored the boxes in a high cupboard.

They prepared a meal, and ate silently, Grandfather's eyebrows heavy.

'I'll clear up,' said Tomlin when they had eaten, and

he left Grandfather at the north window, lighting a cigar, staring from his armchair towards the promontory, and Sequence, full of fish, snoring on a seat.

He set the fishing lines, and pulled in two flounders immediately, little flat flapping plates jittering across the water. He stunned them, and cut one into bait. The seagull came walking on the earth, its bill curved for tearing.

'Don't you have a grandfather to look after you?' asked Tomlin, and the head tilted to let an eye stare at him.

'Maybe you're the grandfather.' He cast with a small rod, whipping the line gently over the ripples. He pushed the cork handle into a cleft, and wound in another flounder from a rod he'd just baited. He drew the hook, and the fish wriggled from his fingers, flip-flopping slapping on the ground, and the gull heaved its wings tiptoeing quickly, dipping its bill, ripping flesh down to the bones while the fish lived.

'Perhaps you're Aunt Bolliter,' said Tomlin.

Grandfather came on to the veranda and went to one of the garden sheds. He brought a green hose to a standpipe, fitted it to the tap, glanced hopefully at the water tank on the caravans, and cried, 'Ha!' as water squealed in the hose, then jetted free. Grandfather wandered, giving drink to the thirsty ground. Tomlin realized the sun was low, though still bright. The fierce heat was gone, and shadows lay soft on the earth.

When he had caught enough fish he reeled in, left the fish bucket in the shade, and while Grandfather gutted the catch, Tomlin staggered with the watering can to areas of the vegetable garden that the hose didn't reach. Then he remembered to haul down the brown and red flags. And he folded them, and stood looking as the sky turned from blue to silver, and the great river lay still with patches dark as glass and even the islands were beautiful; and swifts swung darting after invisible flies, around the flagpole. And the air was a delight to breathe as azaleas released their evening fragrance.

Then he took the flags to their cupboard and lay on his bed, just for a moment, and the sun rolled low towards the north horizon.

❧

When he woke the light had changed, and he knew it was morning. He was still in his shirt and shorts, but his feet were bare and a blanket lay rough on his legs. He went through the house and on to the veranda. Sequence welcomed him with a flap of his tail. Tomlin patted the dog's head respectfully.

He could see Grandfather from the knees up, beyond the orchard, hoeing among the potatoes. He seemed to sink into the earth as he stepped away from Tomlin, working down the slope.

'Grandfather!'

Grandfather paused. He waved and thrust his fingers at his mouth. Tomlin yelled wordlessly and ran to the kitchen. He fried fish, and potato left from yesterday, mashing the potato with a fork, panting, scorching it in the frying pan; making tea black as stout for Grandfather, filling the caravan with tasty smells, hanging himself out the doorway sending his voice piercing

34

through the orchard, and Grandfather's face just visible above the potato slope grinned and his hand popped up beside the grin, waving. And Tomlin rushed to serve the breakfast, plates hot on his palms as he dashed to the table, and they ate, and the sun warmed the island.

'We'll sail,' said Grandfather.

'Oh?'

'North. Up the loch. It's the only way we can bring back food.'

'You don't like sailing.'

Grandfather shook his head grimly. 'We'll put the boat in the water this morning. See it's okay.' He looked out, and the sky hung steadily beyond the window. 'We'll have to wait for a breeze. It's only seven or eight miles.' He gulped his tea. 'Let's get that boat,' he growled.

He strode through the long room and was down the veranda steps with a thud! thud! of his weight on the boards, striding, under the pulley that carried the bean baskets, past the flagpole, to the west shore near the greenhouse. Tomlin running. To the boathouse. Double doors, made of wood, the river lapping below them, shut against the weather; Grandfather's hand-built shore, dipping under the water, forming a slipway. He waded in, unlatched the door sending half back on its hinges towards Tomlin, wading with the other half, fastening it open.

Little rocky stairs took Tomlin past the open door into the boathouse. The floor went round the walls like a very low shelf and the middle was a hollow with the river in it, slapping, echoing, flashing sunlight on to the

35

walls, on to the underside of the boat, for Grandfather's yacht hung above the water, suspended in a cradle of ropes, and the water slop-slapped as Grandfather stood, massive in the enclosing gloom, gigantic beside the dangling hull. Then he turned and his elbows moved in the shadows, and chains clinked as wheels stirred, throwing out a smell of grease, and the great fish-shape jerked towards the water, struck the surface, and Tomlin leapt to release the ropes, hauling them sparkling wet, coiling them on to the floor, while Grandfather leaned on the yacht's little rail, steadying it; and water slapped madly, flickering light into the dimness.

They moored the boat with a line from the prow to an iron ring cemented in the floor. Tyres protected the paint as the hull bumped, sending echoes thudding to the roof.

Grandfather stepped on board, and Tomlin followed, clutching suddenly as the boat wobbled. And Grandfather checked the mast which rested along the length of the boat; checked wire ropes, tutting at rust, nodding at blobs of grease on cleats, oil on metal surfaces, grunting, generally satisfied, Tomlin noticed, with most things, the anchor properly stowed and wedged, plastic paddles.

'It's smaller,' said Tomlin.

Grandfather grinned. 'Or you're bigger,' he said. 'Do you remember – ' His voice rumbled menacingly around the walls, ' – helping me wash salt from the ropes? And we used grease from the drum – ' His head turned and he stared into the gloom. 'There. In the corner. Rescued that from Dixon's garage. And the tyres.' He pressed tyres with his fingers. 'They're lasting well. Come!' he whispered suddenly. 'Into the sunshine! Come!' And Tomlin felt himself half-lifted from the boat, and urged outside, up the shore –

'Look at the sun!' cried Grandfather. 'Feel it! Feel it on your skin! Breathe God's air!' Tomlin screwed his eyes near-shut against the glitter of the sea – the estuary – spreading distantly, hideous islands, the seagull, the mast of the sunken yacht; the hot blue sky turning white at the horizon, the smell of the earth, and the tangy taste of seaweed warming on the beach below the putting green.

'Unless,' said Grandfather, 'a miracle exists some-where on this poor planet – ' He looked down on Tomlin, like mighty Thor in his book from the bookshop, grizzled by war; by surviving. 'Unless there is a miracle,' repeated Grandfather, and Tomlin blinked up at him, 'you are the last human being.'

'You too, Grandfather.'

Grandfather gazed at nothing, then at Tomlin, and his teeth bared savagely. 'I would rage against them!' he bellowed, and a shred of cloud dimmed the sun. 'They grew, generation upon generation! Seeking perfection in everything! Finding it in war! If I had lived among them my fury would have known no end! Better a thousand die, than the whole swarm!' And Grandfath-er's foot raised and struck down, and it seemed to Tomlin that the island dipped and ripples hurried from its shore.

The sun dissolved the cloud, and stared with

white-hot fascination. Then Grandfather's terrible gaze fell on Tomlin and Tomlin's heart beat fast, but Grandfather smiled, sadly. 'Today,' he said, 'we will look at the town. It is time you learned.' He held Tomlin's hand.

'But first, there are chores. I want to check the sail – '

'I'll look for pods!'

Grandfather nodded and Tomlin ran, beginning beneath the bridge; Sequence trotted above the shore; rocks hot, the water smooth and warm on Tomlin's ankles, and distantly, a raft of vegetation, stuck on the wet mirror. Tomlin watched. The vegetation was moving, but so very slightly. In the stillness, Tomlin heard the bees bumbling over the bridge to the greenhouse with its gaping windows; and azaleas flowering around the veranda. Tomlin wondered why Grandfather was so dismayed by the past. He found a pod and held it in his fist.

A hollow flop made him turn. Grandfather on the lawn was shaking out the sail flapping it, tugging it flat, fingering stitches, staring as if remembering. He looked towards Tomlin and waved, and Tomlin waved and searched further, checking rocks and cement, right round to the greenhouse. Then he ran to the veranda rail, took a basket, ran to the pulley, feet up cement steps around the pole, hooked the basket high, threw the pod in the basket, hauled, hauled, dancing the basket along the rope, swaying past Grandfather who gave it a push and grinned at how light it was, pull-and-pause over the carrots and onions, pull-and-pause through the orchard, over the slope of potatoes, small as a sock to the furthest pole. Then he dashed – and Grandfather roared with laughter – to the basket, shoulders under, lift, tip, slither went the pod, plop! sinking into the water. Then he carried the basket back to the rail, and because he was hot he decided Grandfather needed coffee, so he entered the shadow of the house and put the kettle on the gas.

Then he set his little hands to work, peeling potatoes. Cutting them small, boiling them, mashing them, oh, what sore wrists! a drop of precious cooking oil, salt, thump! flat, into the frying pan; mugs, coffee and boil the kettle again! 'Grandfather!'

'Ah!' said Grandfather, clumping to the sink to wash. 'Smells good! Honey?'

'Honey!' gasped Tomlin, and dived to a cupboard for honey-on-the-comb in a clear glass jar, and they went, balancing mugs, potato cakes, and sat at the north window, spooning honey crunchy with wax into thumbed-open cakes, dribbling, laughing, licking fingers, wiping chins, dabbing crumbs, and around them the caravan creaked in the heat, and the island's song was silence.

'Soil,' said Tomlin. 'Soil, Grandfather!'

'Soil,' said Grandfather, raising his eyebrows, sending fingers to scratch at the hair between his shirt buttons. His eyebrows scowled and his lips went into a circle that searched left, then right –

'A cigar!' yelled Tomlin.

'Haw!' cried Grandfather. 'A clever one you are!'

He accepted a cigar, a light from a match, and said, 'Soil. Let me see. Well, in those days machines still functioned. I told you I'd built the island, built the shore to hold the soil. Not only to hold the soil, I wanted it as natural as . . . But the problem was – '

'Mother.'

'Mother?' Grandfather looked startled. 'Yes. Your mother was here. I'd almost forgotten. She was here. While the island grew. Helping. She was younger than you. Quiet. Not like you – '

'Hmn!'

'Red lips and black hair, always close, watching. Stunned, I suppose, at what had happened. She survived the war. For a while. Playing by the stream with another little girl – D'you see? Look. Look!' And Grandfather dabbed his cigar at the window, pointing. 'Where the water comes from that pipe? That's the stream! It's only a pipe under the road. Further up it runs through a gully. That's what saved her. From blast. Radiation. Heat of course. A tree killed her friend.

'There was no warning. I was in the cellar at home watching the mushrooms grow – '

Grandfather closed his mouth tightly. Then he released cigar smoke, and blinked rather a lot, his eyes watering, and he drummed his mug on the table. 'Your Grandmother – I haven't told you. She was like me. Strong. Just as clever. Y'know how clever your old Grandad is – ? A blast of light. Oh, such light! Can you look into the sun! Imagine the sun's light if you stared into it – but all around! Even in the darkness of the cellar, down two flights of stairs and the great stone house above, and yet came the light, blinding, making me scream in fear for I knew what it was, knew I could do nothing! And the heat came! Oh, the horror! Ancient timbers simply exploded with fire, the bulb above the stairway melted, and I saw nothing more for the blast dropped a piece of the house over me, protecting me – though not protecting my imagination, for I knew what was happening on the ground. That my town was being blown away. The people of my town shrivelled into ash, cars and buses melted into pools of metal, into gas, the waters of this estuary boiled into the sky . . . Armageddon.'

Grandfather's hand trembled around his coffee. 'No one could describe it properly. The smells. Horror. Created by nature's most spiritual being. People eating. People talking to neighbours. People going to work. Owning cats and dogs. Riding horses. Sailing. Watching television. Shopping. Going to the dentist. And other people, planning how to kill them. Killing them. Thirty-thousand people to the north of the bomb. Who knows how many others? Is there anyone left who could know?

'A few survived. Over a hundred. Especially at the far end of town – where your mother was. We were really on the edge of the blast. I expected more bombs, but nothing else happened. Except that the town burned. Then it rained. Rain like you have never seen. If I hadn't escaped from the cellar I would have drowned. Your mother nearly did drown. But I got to her in time. Though I could hardly see for smoke, and steam rising from the hot ground. The rain was the river returning.'

Grandfather wept.

He drank the rest of his coffee, blew his nose, relit his cigar, blinked, sighed.

'You don't have to tell me any more,' whispered Tomlin.

'Oh. I think I do. I think it's time. Yes. Well. The survivors. Most of them died within a few hours. I tried to gather them together. But people were so shocked. Some didn't want to live. In places you couldn't tell where houses had been, where the streets were. And strange shadows at the north end where walls still stood – oh, Tomlin! the horror! The horror of a wall with the shadow of a woman, a pale shadow on a burnt wall! or the shape of a tree. Little trees that decorated the grass verges, but they were incinerated instantly, their patterns printed on stone. One still survives. Am I making sense? I mean a person. One survivor – '

'You, Grandfather?' whispered Tomlin.

'Margrit Bolliter,' said Grandfather. 'The rest are gone – '

'The Poor Souls – ?'

'They are children of survivors. The rest are gone. Your mother. Your father – no more! If only I had existed sooner – !'

Tomlin gazed at his grandfather, not understanding.

'What do you mean?'

'What do I mean?' cried Grandfather, and Sequence, who lay at the kitchen end of the long room, raised his head, suddenly. Grandfather's mouth gaped, but instead of speaking, he closed his lips over his cigar. 'I will tell you one day what I mean.' His blue eyes nailed Tomlin to his seat. 'One day you will know. But not yet.

There are other things to know first. Things to see. Things to realize. Only then, perhaps, will you understand why I say that I should have lived sooner. Haw! I was going to tell you the story of the soil! But there! My cigar is finished. Your coffee finished?'

Tomlin gulped at his mug and nodded.

Grandfather stood up, his white hair touching the roof of the caravan. 'We will go into the town.'

'The town!'

'Just to see how truthful Margrit is.'

'But – '

'I know. The shops are hers and the river ours. We won't tell her, eh?' And Grandfather's eye closed in a wink. 'There are places you should see. Yes. Places you must see. Places you must remember. Come! Come! Come! Get ready! Up!'

'Socks and shoes?'

'Socks and shoes!' cried Grandfather, and he reached for the cupboard where his whip hung curled on a hook. Tomlin rushed to his bedroom, pulled on socks, slipped into shoes, dashed to the toilet, ran to find Grandfather and Sequence waiting at the bridge. 'Do you think,' cried Tomlin, 'the Poor Souls will have enough fish?' He stared towards the shadows between the church and tall buildings.

'I don't think Aunt Bolliter will go short,' said Grandfather, and Tomlin looked at him, wondering at the coldness in his voice. 'Come!'

Across the bridge. Water lying in silken ripples. Farewell to the bees from Grandfather. Then they went across the shore road with its hard dry weeds and

43

scattered trees, up the first avenue away from the water, crunching, rustling through vegetation, Tomlin sneezing in dust, Sequence sneezing into his whiskers, houses watching, unblinking in the sunlight, hard shadows standing inside, or bright day behind windows where walls stood roofless; trees everywhere; rubble underfoot, black from a dreadful scorching; glass melted into wonderful shapes; sharp stacks of metal and rust with rubber tyres crumbling; and everywhere, insects flickering, buzzing, birds flitting, trees in flower –

'Listen.'

They listened. Chirrup.

Hum and buzz. And the gurgle of water.

'There's a lot of life,' said Grandfather, and his voice rose hopefully. 'But the stream.' And he marched on, the whip curled in his fist.

Houses. Once grand. 'A rich town!' cried Grandfather suddenly, and a blackbird raced under a privet, clucking warnings. 'Now your carpets are food for mould! And the worm consumes the ashes of your furniture! And because of fools you are wiped away in a breath of air hotter than the surface of the sun!'

He strode with weed-crushing force to a doorway, through the doorway, testing beams, beam-stepping, striding in sunlight in pink-flowering weeds through someone's dining room, Tomlin following, Sequence sitting, tongue dripping. 'This way!' cried Grandfather, and Tomlin heard the voice of water.

He stopped beside Grandfather, and Grandfather's five fingers dug into his shoulder, and they looked on a

44

little ravine, weed-solid, trees leaning, birds rustling, and beneath, unseen gurgling water.

Grandfather's fingers relaxed. 'I don't recognize it,' he breathed, and a column of midges shifted among shadows like dust sparkling. Grandfather turned. 'I think . . . Oh, how memory deceives! Or is it so changed?' He stepped among rubble, seeing something, reaching weed-deep, lifting, in a burst of grass seed, a lion's head, a stone roar, the jaws sprouting daisies, carved eyes blind towards the sun.

'This is the place,' murmured Grandfather. He turned again to the ravine. 'Even the fallen tree is gone. She must still be there. Your mother's little friend.'

Silence, with weeds and trees motionless, a buttercup nodding with a bee in its mouth. The column of midges rising and falling in strange patterns of movement. Gurgle, gurgle, said the stream, and deep, deep in the undergrowth, a girl's bones; worth nothing but chemicals for searching roots. 'Would they have dropped their bomb,' said Grandfather, 'if they'd looked into this child's face? Oh, just a little bit of thought! Just a moment's consideration!' His voice rose among branches. 'Was this child your enemy?' But the silence made no reply and the stream gurgled on and the plants sought bones for food. 'Come!' whispered Grandfather. 'There is more.'

They stumbled among rubble to where Sequence sprawled in the shade of leaves. Tomlin rubbed his tummy and the dog struggled up and panted as they walked east, away from the water.

'The blast came from the south,' said Grandfather,

pointing right. 'See these red sandstone blocks at your feet? They're part of that house. And this chimney pot. Isn't it big! What craftsmanship! What love! in making something to perch so high the detail can't be seen! See – ' He turned the pot with his foot and it fell apart. 'That side was towards the heat.' And Tomlin stared at the black molten surface, not sure that he understood. It was difficult to think that the world had ever been different. He tried to imagine the houses whole, as he had seen in books, and people inside, and coming out to sit in cars, to drive – but all he could see was tumbled stone and thriving nature.

They clambered, Sequence waiting to be carried over the worst rubble; watched by tall trees, scratched by short trees, white moths rising, bees and darting birds, and the sun hammered mercilessly, making them pause in the shade, sweating, snatching hands from stone too hot to lean on.

East. To the Victorian school with its pillared entrance sheltered from the blast, and iron hinges hanging, the door long burnt away or rotted; the floor protected by tiles intact, but creaking, and shadows filling corridors, hanging in the assembly hall; plaques and photographs surviving on the walls, lines of faces grinning above school ties, rows of ears printed by the camera.

'Spiders,' whispered Tomlin, wiping web from his fingers on to his socks. He followed Grandfather who pushed a door, and they stared into a classroom.

For a long time Grandfather didn't speak.

Desks stood neat and dusty, one or two collapsing.

A blackboard with the estuary mapped in chalk, and writing, faint under grime.

'Your mother sat there,' whispered Grandfather. He walked in and looked down at a desk. 'I heard them singing once. Can you imagine? A little voice like yours –'

Tomlin tilted his head as if to listen, and Sequence lay gasping.

' – and other young voices, all singing, ringing round the ceiling, faces mouthing, can you imagine? ringing, hearts surging in their bodies; breathing, soaring their songs in joy at being alive, watching the beat of the teacher's hand! Beat! Beat! Louder! Louder! Quieter, quieter, melody low, beat, beat, sing it higher! Then –' Grandfather stood very straight. He sighed. 'Then they went home, one black Friday, and died.'

He raised the lid of the desk just a finger's width, two fingers' width; then lowered it, shut it, held it down.

But they lingered, Grandfather and Tomlin; listened to imagined singing. Feet clattering, reprimands, laughter. Then the silence. And birds squeezing out their summer music. Tomlin pushed his fingers into Grandfather's hand. He had never known loneliness.

Then they returned to the sunshine, and Tomlin screwed his face against the brightness, and peered, startled, as Grandfather laughed.

'Grandfather?'

'There's just a chance – !' cried Grandfather, and went back between the pillars, leaving Tomlin. But Sequence was not enough company, even for a minute, and Tomlin followed, over the tiles, stood in a doorway,

Grandfather very still in a small room, facing a grand desk, facing horror that grinned from the chair; a face of bones; hands of bones; strange clothes, the outer garment black and enfolding like bat's wings, but dusty, all dropping apart. Then Grandfather moved. Round the desk, pushing away the chair letting the headmaster collapse into dust, sliding drawers, clicking open a cupboard, smiling, seeing Tomlin, showing him two bottles, one almost full.

'Brandy?'

'Brandy!' cried Grandfather waving the full bottle. 'And whisky. That rascal – ' He wagged the whip at the chair, ' – never went short. Hard to believe he was as fat as Bolliter! Haw! Haw! Well! Well.' He gazed around. 'Well. I never thought,' he murmured, 'last time I was here, that I'd see this. Hmm. Let's get out.'

Grandfather pointed with the whip, and across a vast sprawl of rubble Tomlin saw the Plant, a green fringe apparently harmless, apparently waiting. 'But it's not waiting!' cried Grandfather. 'It's closer every time a pod falls. And don't they fall when it rains! Don't we catch them in our baskets! ha! drown them! keeping them off our island.'

He found a stone in the shade of a laburnum and sat on it, and Tomlin sat, with Sequence panting. 'That's the real killer,' gasped Grandfather, waving towards the Plant. 'Eating the landscape. I wish we'd brought some water. This stuff's no use for a thirst.' He balanced the bottles among stones and weeds. 'It was a long time before I realized why more bombs didn't fall. Millions survived, y'know. Must'v'done. The Plant wiped them out. *We* started it. Some lunatic pressed the button. Three and one-sixth minutes later, Eastern Europe, Russia covered in white spots of light and winds carrying radioactive earth and water, dust, powdered people spreading death. That's why so few bombs fell here. The Plant was slower, but just as deadly. Did I ever tell you about sleeping in the Plant? No? No. Well. Later maybe. Let's move on, eh? The memories come rolling back.' He stood up.

'What's that on the stone, Grandfather?' said Tomlin.

Grandfather turned his seat over, and a metal plate, rusted into holes, said NORFOLK STREET.

'Norfolk Street,' murmured Grandfather. 'I knew people who lived in Norfolk Street. The Graysons. Mad about cats. Ha. Oh. Come on. We've got to get to the shops. Back to the water. Come on, you old dog!' he told Sequence. 'Maybe we'll find you a puddle to wet your tongue!' And Grandfather wiped sweat from his face with the back of his hand, crinkled his cheeks at the sky, and muttered, 'Fat chance!'

They went on. Finding a wending way among old gardens, shaded by trees. Grandfather wondering out loud at the many birds; and grinning, pointing the whip, gripping Tomlin's head to point his face towards movement in the grass; tiny brown haunches with a wandering tail; and they passed, delighted at seeing a mouse; for a mouse was Life.

Once, Sequence trotted, whuffing in his whiskers, down a slope, lap lapping, and Grandfather with

49

Tomlin, went beside him, crouching, hands breaking the stream's surface, drinking – 'It's not very nice, Grandfather' – but wet, sending them cheerfully forward.

Eventually, they came to a door in a roughcast wall. A wide door that opened down the middle, with a metal hasp and a padlock.

'Is this the shop?' whispered Tomlin jiggling the padlock. 'It's greasy,' he complained, finding brown jelly sticky on his fingers.

Grandfather's head turned making Tomlin look away. Something banged and there was the padlock open, and Grandfather lifting it from the hasp. 'Grandfather –'

The door scraped over weeds, and shadows invited them in. Tomlin peered, dazzled, seeing shapes, seeing Grandfather moving quickly, shifting a box, tilting a box. 'Plenty of soap powder,' he breathed. 'Peas. Marrowfat peas. We've got peas, haven't we?'

'Yes –'

'No tinned fruit. No beans. What's this? Spaghetti? Spaghetti! Spaghetti!' Grandfather's voice rattled around shelves. 'We'll take a box of this!'

'But Grandfather!'

'Mm? What? What! She swore there was none! All these years! None left, she said! That's what I *mean*! Some people take and take – !'

'But it's not ours, Grandfather!'

'We agreed to trade, Tomlin. We agreed the river is ours, the town hers. But she is cheating –'

'It's not ours.'

Grandfather rested the box. He looked all around. Looked at the ceiling. The floor. Sighed. Left the box. 'Right,' he said. 'But let's see what else is here. Then we'll know what we're bargaining for.' And he prowled, growling, and Sequence followed. There wasn't much.

'So,' said Grandfather. 'The back shop is empty. Very nearly. We'll try . . .' His voice faded, '. . . the front shop. Where is the door to the front shop? Where is the door!' he cried, and shadows stood still among the shelves. Grandfather stared again at the floor. 'She keeps it clean. She's been here, that Bolliter! That Margrit. The Poor Souls wouldn't have cleaned it without her here to tell them. But look at the tiles.'

And Tomlin looked. Rubber tiles. Well swept. Worn by many feet, curled and crumbled. The bottles tinkled in Grandfather's left hand. He waved the whip at the floor. 'Well?'

'It's clean,' said Tomlin.

'It's worn,' said Grandfather. 'Mostly here.' He marched to the door they'd come in, and stomped. 'And there.' He pointed, and followed his pointing arm to the stack of soap powder and spaghetti. 'Isn't it odd that the worn tiles go under these boxes?'

'I – '

'Of course it isn't. Because Margrit Bolliter has hidden the door behind the boxes. And she has hidden the door to keep me out. To keep us out.'

'But – '

'We will discover why.' And Grandfather smiled as he placed the bottles on a shelf. He handed Tomlin the whip, eased his fingers into the pile of boxes, lifted four boxes, smiling, teeth showing just a little, placed the boxes on the floor. Tomlin laid the whip around the bottles, gripped one box, pulled, it slid, pulled-slid – 'Oh!' he leapt as the box dived at his feet, crumpled its nose on the tiles.

Grandfather's hands swept the box away, worked on, astonishing Tomlin with his strength, exposing a double rubber door. And they clambered over boxes and stood in darkness cut by threads of sunlight;

the smell of rubber and soap powder. 'She's blocked the windows,' murmured Grandfather. 'So no one can see in. There's no one here but us,' he added. 'Well.'

'Well,' said Tomlin. He looked back for Sequence, and heard panting in the back shop. Dark towers of cardboard rose around him.

'Well,' said Grandfather again.

'There's not much on the shelves,' whispered Tomlin. 'Look at all those boxes.'

They walked among the towers. Tomlin finding Grandfather's hand. Bumping stockinged legs. Seeing better by the sun-bright slits between boards that covered the windows. Such odd smells. And cold shelves. Cool jars of jam and honey still on display, tempting ghosts.

'So,' said Grandfather. They kept walking. Round the whole shop.

'My, my,' said Grandfather. 'Goodness.'

They went out, replacing the spaghetti and soap powder; out to the sunlight. Replacing the padlock. Grandfather looking at the grease on his hands, Tomlin clutching the bottles and the whip.

They went away from the shop, on to the shore road, and found steps around the monument. Grandfather sat in the shade lighting a cigar from his little tin, shaking out the match, gazing towards the shadow of the church.

'I saw her kill a man,' said Grandfather, and Tomlin, watching a bee nosing into the scarlet cup of a poppy, stared.

Grandfather's head leaned back on the monument, his cigar at an angle, blue smoke spindling into the air. 'She was always strong. Played tennis, before the war. Swimming. Competing. Always wanting to be best. When there was hardly anyone left – your mother was dead. Your father . . . Well.

'There was me. But she never understood me. Stayed beside me a lot, but always . . . watching. Jim Park she didn't watch. Jim was useful. Good with machines, and she didn't like people cleverer than herself, and he turned his back on her and she finished him with a brick. Wham!'

Grandfather turned the cigar in his fingers, cast a glance at Tomlin. 'It's not pleasant. It's not. But you must learn. You're cleverer than she is. We can't blame her entirely. Not entirely – the bomb made quite a few people mad. But we're cleverer than she is. I wonder if she's decided to use a brick on us.'

'Grandfather!'

Grandfather's blue eyes slid round on Tomlin.

'Grandfather, what do you mean!'

'I think she wants to kill us.'

Beyond the poppies, the sea glittered. The bee climbed to the poppy's lip, soared, settled on another scarlet cup. Sequence crawled further into the shade as the sun touched his back.

'Couldn't you have stopped her?'

'Stopped her! When three people are together and one lifts a brick you do not think someone's about to be murdered. Even when she held it above her head, it didn't dawn on me. She smiled! "Jim!" she said. He turned. *Wham!*'

'Wham.'

'Wham,' sighed Grandfather.

The water sparkled.

'Weren't you angry?'

'I didn't believe it. Couldn't. She wandered off, smiling, I think. She was top of the heap, then. Except for me. I couldn't believe she'd done it.'

'Didn't you want to kill her?'

'Killing is wrong.'

Tomlim peered into the glitter of water at the island, its pattern of vegetables neat, green and bright, azaleas splashing colours in the shadow of the house, and the flagpole bare like the monument at his back. He stood up, up a step, round to the sunshine surface of the monument, feeling the lettering cut in granite. TO THE MEMORY OF THE MEN WHO GAVE THEIR LIVES IN THE SECOND WORLD WAR 1939–1945. He sighed and returned to the shade, close to Grandfather, leaning his cheek on the shirt sleeve, clutching the arm, fingering the skin, hair curving outward like a meadow of grey grass, and rivers of blue, feeding the flesh.

'What will she do?'

'Do? Well.' Grandfather's glance slid down on Tomlin. 'Well. Who knows? Let's see. She told us she had no food. Did she mean it?'

'There's lots – !'

'Lots! Yes. But maybe ... maybe there used to be much more and what we saw is just a little to Margrit, and she really was worried – or she knows there is plenty and wanted us to ... Hmn,' said Grandfather.

'Wanted us to what, Grandfather?'

'I was going to say, "wanted us to take the boat out". But I suggested that. Unless she guessed I would. Is she that clever? Telling us there's no food, hoping I would say we'd take the boat; she knows I can't swim. D'you think she's that clever! How long did she take – !' shouted Grandfather along the shore road, ' – to think this up!'

'Grandfather!'

'Well. She took a long time to store the boxes in the shop. She came out to do that. What an effort to come out! They carry her, you know. Like an empress. Wobbling on a chair for all the world to see! Except there are no eyes left. Then the Poor Souls struggling, laden with boxes, from this little shop and that little shop, stacking cardboard in the shadows, nailing up the windows. Can you see them using a hammer and nails? Good thing they have few fingers to hurt. Then she calls on me and says there is no food and I say I will take the boat ... ' Grandfather stubbed out his cigar, gathered the whip and bottles. 'Is she that clever?' He rose leaving Tomlin sitting looking up; Grandfather's face

sad and grim. 'Is she beginning another war?' he asked.
And water rippled beyond the putting green and the
smell of seaweed wrinkled Tomlin's nose.

They returned to the island, murmuring at the bees,
silence between them, Sequence squarely patient,
waiting for fish; a meal at the north window, Grandfather's eye crinkled against the sun, thinking, saw
Tomlin. Margrit Bolliter in his head.

※

The little boat wobbled in the water. Tomlin checked
again that he'd tied the painter to the cement stump. He
felt the plastic bag, hoping he'd packed enough potato
cakes, wondering which Poor Soul Margrit would send.
Grandfather had signalled for only one, his five-
fingered hands sending the flag soaring to the flagpole's
tip, hanging black – one flag, one person.

Moisture, saw Tomlin, already beaded the inside of
the bag, the cakes sweating in the early sun, oozing
honey – some of them – or fish paste; fish beaten with
chives and drops of sweet oil by Grandfather's swift
wrist, light and tasty; and others, fat with jam from last
year's plum crop. And a bottle of water.

Plop! said the river, squashed between the boat and
the island, plop! wobbling as Grandfather stepped the
mast, pointing it at God in the sky, rattling the wire
ropes, back bent, hands out for the bag and bottle,
ducking into the little cabin, hands out for the knife,
'Careful!' at Tomlin, and Tomlin using all six fingers to
pass the terrible thing across the plopping water, holding the handle, the handle, oak, hard, once the leg of a

table, cut to fit Grandfather's mighty grip, bound with leather, tight, and the blade swinging heavy, a thick back edge, and a cutting edge that could slice a dropping feather.

'Here it comes,' said Grandfather, and Tomlin turned seeing a figure proceeding on the shore road, trudging.

'Pick,' said Grandfather in a voice that made Tomlin stare. 'Stay by me,' said Grandfather gently. 'Not by him. Pick is the strongest. He can talk. He can remember. He remembers instructions.'

Tomlin watched as the Poor Soul came through the trees, among the weeds. He stomped over the lawn and stood very still by the bridge, head dipped.

Grandfather pulled the painter, until the boat was a step from the shore. He strode on to the island, hand on the stump, gathering the curl of whip from beside Tomlin's foot, anger in his stride, on to the bridge, Tomlin running, Sequence trotting; towards the Poor Soul;

and the Poor Soul stood still;

head dipped, like the seagull, one eye brown and watching, the other white, quite blind; bees climbing his cheek, buzzing airborne, returning, clambering over his skull through hair as limp as string; bees on his hands counting the fingers; fur spots on his white shirt crawling upwards; bees making him stand still.

'Pick,' said Grandfather softly.

The eye stared, but a bee on his lip kept him silent.

Grandfather went close. Tomlin watched. Grandfather walked around Pick, his shoulder near the one-eyed face, right round behind, grinning unhappily at the bees in the string. Pick's white eye slipped vainly,

57

mocking the brown, imitating the good eye.

'Your heart is not true,' said Grandfather. 'Don't you know,' he whispered, 'don't you know? Don't you know! the bees see a man's thoughts? and they dance a warning on his skin, singing, singing with their wings, dancing to their song, warning! warning! Pick! warning the dark heart, Pick!'

Grandfather was silent, suddenly; and Pick's eye retreated, it seemed, behind the eyelid, defeated before his war had begun, and the bee left his lip; bees rose from his hair, his hands, his white shirt, spotless. 'Welcome,' said Grandfather, his voice as gentle as the swish of his whip. 'Come.' And he gestured Pick on to the bridge, and behind his back, said 'Thank you' to the bees. 'Thank you, thank you.'

Pick went, feet hollow on the metal path, Grandfather, Sequence and Tomlin following, tick-tick of Sequence's claws, Tomlin trying to walk as silent as a grandfather, grasping an imaginary whip, bulging imaginary muscles. No one was as strong as Grandfather.

On the little boat the boom swung fat with the sail taped round it; the mast tipped naked as the water moved, rocking, jerking as Pick clumped on board, sitting quickly at Grandfather's command; and Grandfather sat holding a paddle, showing Pick the grip, and Sequence hopped, his back-end aided by Tomlin.

'Tell the bees,' said Grandfather, and he nodded encouragingly as Tomlin hesitated. 'Tell them we'll be gone most of the day. You know!'

And Tomlin ran, drum-drum on the path, patter on the bridge. 'And put something on your feet!' yelled

Grandfather, making Tomlin hesitate again, but he went among the bees, the grass crisp on his soles. A bee crawled on his arm.

'We're going north,' breathed Tomlin. 'North! Grand-father and Sequence and me. Most of the day. It may be evening before we come back. Please look after the island. Buzz, buzz. Thank you!' And the bee rose, letting Tomlin run to the house for canvas shoes, socks tucked in them, shoes dumped into the boat, painter untied from the concrete stump, push the boat off, jump, bump and stumble on to the thwart.

'Take the tiller, Mr Tomlin!'

'Aye, aye, Cap'n!'

And the water broke as paddles dug the surface and the hull pressed the blue liquid aside, gurgling under the stern, burbling around the rudder, and the island slid away remarkably fast.

The sun watched, raising itself higher for a better look, warming the rail around the little boat, sparkling on the rigging, swelling blobs of dazzle on the water, making Tomlin blink.

'Steer clear of the promontory,' ordered Grandfather, his back bending in time with Pick as they dipped paddles and pulled. The promontory swung close to starboard and Tomlin stared at the Plant, writhing, it seemed, but not moving, a crowd, thought Tomlin, of green people quietly strangling each other.

They passed the promontory, and hills rose, swollen with the Plant, enclosing the loch, mirrored in the still water.

'Pull!' urged Grandfather as Pick struck the paddle

deep. 'Pull! We're skipping along! Soon be there. Dip! Pull! This is fun!' and Tomlin saw Pick's head turn towards Grandfather. 'Pull!' from Grandfather. Pick's back spreading wide as he leaned into the stroke, but his white eye wobbling at Grandfather. 'Well done! Speeding along! All this!' he cried, and Tomlin saw one ear then the other as Grandfather regarded the hills. 'All this! With pretty houses above the shore! All the way round almost! Except where the submarine base was, and it was ugly. Flat-faced buildings and a giant dry dock tall as a tree, long as a street! Y'could still see it last time I was here. See it again soon at this speed. Follow the curve of the shore, Mister Mate!'

'Aye, aye, Cap'n!'

'And trees, Pick! D'y'like trees? Aren't they just beautiful? Thousands of them, and high on the hills, heather, gorse and grass, and purple rock at the peaks. Beautiful! Beautiful! Keep in time. Stroke. Pull! Good. Stroke. Pull. Now it's all this horrible Plant. Not too hot are y'Pick? Stroke. Pull. Sweating a bit, eh? Won't worry a strong man like you, eh? That's what comes of killing people. The Plant. The Plant comes. Fools blasting the world with radiation. We mustn't kill, Pick. Never kill. Not me! Not the boy – '

Pick's blind eye (which had turned away and back many times as Grandfather talked) turned again and wrinkled itself inside the skin of eyelids, and wobbled horribly like a pea bleached by the sun.

' – not a bird, nor mouse!' bellowed Grandfather. 'We can't replace them! Keep paddling, Pick! Don't pause! You'll have us in circles!'

Tomlin struggled with the tiller as the boat curved. He glanced back, and saw the wake swerving, then curving again as Pick dipped and pulled, and Grandfather matched the stroke; then the wake settled to a spreading skirt with pairs of churning patches where the paddles had struck. And Tomlin imagined the waves of the little craft patting the shore a mile off, clapping on rocks below the reach of their vegetable enemy.

But on the near shore, Tomlin spied concrete poles, sadly bent-headed above the Plant, and he called out to Grandfather.

'That's the road to where we're going. Lampposts, boy! That's the shore road! The same road beside the putting green. On it goes! Miles of it! More miles than you can imagine. And packed with traffic from the base! Cars and buses, solid from here to there – ' Grandfather's head gestured the full length of the loch, ' – full of living people. Hundreds and hundreds of people. All alive! Twice a day rushing along that road! No Plant to stop them. No politician deciding they should burn to death! Someone decided that, you know! Someone decided! Someone had to say to himself, ALL THESE PEOPLE WILL DIE TODAY BECAUSE I THINK THEY SHOULD! Can you imagine!' Grandfather's face swung towards Pick, and though no sound broke the hot day but the rush of water, Grandfather bellowed as if the Poor Soul were deaf. 'You would need to be awfully clever to know when thousands of people should die! I'm glad I'm not that clever! Are you that clever, Pick!' Grandfather stopped paddling and his fingers caught Pick's arm and dribbles dimpled the water as the paddles rested.

Tomlin watched the white pea of Pick's eye flicker on Grandfather, and Grandfather's eye, blue as the summer water, steady, and Grandfather grinned saying again, 'Are you that clever, Pick? Are you clever enough to know when I should die?'

Silence crept out around the little boat, *plop*, said the water. Over the rippled face of the loch, the mirrored Plant wrinkled, silence vast among the hills, and God, thought Tomlin, leaned down to hear the man's reply.

Pick's mouth opened. Bristles clustered in the creases of his cheeks where his razor had swept by. His tongue pushed out the words: 'Aunt Bolliter! Is clever! She says – ' The pea in his eyelids danced.

'She says what?' growled Grandfather.

'Not to tell.'

'Is she clever enough to tell when I should die?'

Pick nodded.

'But am I not cleverer than Aunt Bolliter?'

Nodding.

'And I say that I should not die.'

Pick sat still, rocking slightly as ripples heaved the boat. Thinking. 'Aunt Bolliter . . . ' He dropped his paddle with a clatter that filled the loch for an instant. His left arm came up and Tomlin blinked, astonished – wondering if he'd shut his eyes for a second or two seconds – for Grandfather's five fingers, without seeming to move, were on Pick's throat; then Pick was still again, and Grandfather a statue, like the mighty Laocöon in Tomlin's book, but with a shirt and ancient hair and eyebrows.

Then Pick turned his left arm, bared his arm for

Grandfather to see, and Grandfather's fingers relaxed.

'You are afraid of Aunt Bolliter,' he said, and Tomlin sighed with annoyance, remembering Rem and diamond knuckles thudding making Rem weep.

'Take your paddle,' said Grandfather. 'Stroke. Pull. Stroke. Pull. Stroke . . .' Up the loch, patterning the water with churned-up dapples. Stroke. Pull. Rotting yachts on the shore buried in sand, crows flapping on the beach. Round a curve of rock. 'There!' said Grandfather. And they advanced, wondering, on a rust-red structure, higher than trees, flat walls of metal, panels leaning loose, metal bones naked searching the sky, and along the walls, skirts of seaweed, black-green. And as they passed, water, pushed out from their little yacht, slopped, echoing slightly between the metal cliffs and the water's surface, then Grandfather pointed again, and Tomlin saw, with disgust, a finger of the Plant projecting out from shore.

'That's where we're heading,' said Grandfather, and Tomlin eased the tiller, pointing the boat landwards. 'That was the pier. Timber. Well creosoted. The Plant's making a meal of it though!' And Tomlin saw that the Plant on the pier was smaller than usual, perhaps as high as his shoulder, and thinner, and much of the timber was untouched.

'The village is past the pier!' cried Grandfather.

Tomlin steered around, and saw the village, deep in heavy greenery and awful white flowers; and the beach encircled the water.

'The head of the loch!' cried Pick suddenly and Grandfather looked at him.

'The head of the loch,' agreed Grandfather. 'Well done. Good. Take us on to the sand,' he ordered Tomlin, and Tomlin leaned on the tiller, the paddles rested, they slid forward, crunching gently, the keel nuzzling sand beneath the water, and the boat stopped, rocking a little, floating.

'She'll be all right,' said Grandfather. 'Tide's coming in. But we'll have to wade ashore.' He descended into the cabin and returned with the knife and whip. 'Pick, bring the anchor. Tie there.' And Grandfather and Tomlin watched as the Poor Soul knotted the rope slowly but securely; then they waded ashore, Tomlin supporting Sequence as the dog struggled to swim, and Grandfather talking to Pick, explaining; and Pick struck the anchor's fluke into the sand above the high-tide mark, among the roots of the Plant.

Tomlin's bare feet burned on grit, cooled on grey mud. His socks and shoes lay in the boat. The Plant fringed the shore, its trunks smoothly green, growing so crammed that Tomlin's arm could scarcely have found a gap between.

'Grandfather – ' said Tomlin.

'Stand back,' said Grandfather, and he gazed up the sloping shore, over the Plant. 'There's a roof. It's very low.' He stepped close to the Plant, and a fan of light spread from his hand as the sun caught the sweep of the great knife *slice!* whispered the knife and a trunk – stout as a man's body – slid; sap bled like thick water, but the trunk stayed supported by other trunks and curling tendrils. Light fanned again, and two trunks slid, pouring sap *slice!* more trunks leaned; then the blade flickered above Grandfather's head, and dropped swiftly, shearing, tendrils springing; trunks sagging, like weary green people, on to the beach.

'Pull them away,' said Grandfather, and Pick dragged the bodies aside, tasting the juice on his hands; spitting. And Grandfather advanced, the blade splitting the air with light, cutting the Plant with razor swiftness; Pick bending, hauling the tangled dead below the tide mark.

And the sun sailed high over the loch hot with interest on Grandfather's back, sweat on Grandfather's neck, sweat and the Plant's wet blood on his arm; sweeping the steel, stepping, stump-stepping, slipping on the oozing juice –

Resting.

Panting.

Grinning round at Tomlin, crinkling an eye, crying a word of praise to Pick, and Pick nodding happily. Then on, the mighty blade biting a path, the Plant weeping away its pale blood, a huddled crowd, green, and too clinging to retreat.

Then Pick hauled aside the Plant, revealing the low roof. It was low, saw Tomlin, because it rested on a pile of sand mingled with roots of the Plant.

'See!' panted Grandfather, 'what the Plant does to stone and wood!' He let the sand drain between his fingers. 'All that's left of someone's house. In a few months the roof will be gone.'

'It doesn't like slates,' said Tomlin.

Grandfather's head moved. 'You're right.' He lifted slates from between the stumps. 'Untouched,' he said. 'It doesn't like slates,' he told Pick.

'But what does it mean, Grandfather?'

'Anything the Plant doesn't like must be remembered,' said Grandfather. 'Water.'

'I didn't bring it! I'll get it!' Tomlin dashed from under Grandfather's gaze, the loch washing juice from his feet as he waded, pulled himself over the boat's bow, down dripping into the cabin, finding the bottle, plunging towards the shore again, through the rising tide; Grandfather flipping the top from the bottle, rim at his lips, pausing; grinning suddenly and pushing the bottle to the Poor Soul who gaped, then guzzled the glass until Grandfather cried, 'Enough!' Then Grandfather drank and Tomlin drank. Tomlin closed the bottle and watched Grandfather go up the roof and look down on the Plant, his back turned.

'The road was here,' said Grandfather. 'Come up. Throw the bottle. Sequence, stay! Come on, Pick!' And they sped up the roof and looked at the village.

Tomlin could see where the road had wound around the curve of the loch, for the Plant grew thin on the road, no higher than his shoulder, its flowers sickly, the white petals tipped brown, and space to walk between the trunks.

'It doesn't like tarmac,' murmured Grandfather. 'Tar and creosote.'

'Slate!' said Pick.

'You do listen!' laughed Grandfather. 'We could make something of this one! Eh, Tomlin?' And he grinned at Tomlin, nodded towards Pick, and Pick smiled, his pea eye disappearing, his face suddenly hopeful.

'Grandfather,' said Tomlin. 'The tiles are burning my feet.'

'Shoes in the boat, eh? Down we go then. Take the bottle.' Down went Grandfather on the slope of tiles, stepping on to the Plant, slicing away the tops, walking on the stronger trunks, and Tomlin followed, slipping, but sliding comfortably on the smooth green limbs; Pick laughing, and Tomlin turned to see Pick screwing up his face at a giant flower, his fingers on the flower's stem making it wobble in return. Tomlin laughed, touching Grandfather, and Grandfather smiled, then led them down among the thinly growing Plant on the road.

'This way!' Grandfather took them across the road. Glass facing them, reflecting their three faces, reflecting the Plant behind them, darkness beyond the glass and a brick wall around the shop window, beginning to crumble; a door shut neat tight in the doorway, green paint curling, green shoots of the Plant curling among the paint. Grandfather tugged the handle and stepped back as the door crumbled, dust wafting up. He showed Tomlin and Pick the metal handle in his hand.

'Wait,' said Grandfather, as Tomlin moved. Grandfather prodded the bricks. 'All right. The floor may be eaten,' he warned, and felt with his foot, weight on his step, into the shadows of the shop.

And the shadows stared, it seemed to Tomlin, hiding behind beams of sunlight.

A trickle of dust dripped past Tomlin, piling at his foot. He glanced up but saw only blotched darkness after the daylight. He followed Grandfather and Pick around the shelves. 'Not much,' said Pick.

'Not much,' agreed Grandfather with a sigh. 'I am sure Margrit won't starve. It smells,' he growled.

Tomlin heard dust trickle again.

'The back shop is there,' said Grandfather, but he stood still. Tomlin saw he held Pick's arm.

'Grandfather –'

'Not much here,' said Grandfather and he stared at Tomlin in the gloom, and Pick's head tipped as he looked into the shadows with his one eye.

Tomlin stared where the dust had dribbled. It seemed that the silence was no longer silence, but a sly shuffling and voices in a dream; but neither Pick nor Grandfather stirred. Above the dribble, rafters cut dark lines in the gloom, and on one rose pale shapes, unmoving. The dust hanging in a column reminded Tomlin of midges; but not alive.

And the murmurings shifted around the walls; and shufflings, slight as mice, pattered under shelves; from tin to tin, corner to dark corner.

Tomlin wished Sequence was with him, woolly against his leg, panting, eyebrows twitching, searching out the cause of these horrid noises.

From Grandfather's right hand the thong of the whip uncurled towards the floor, and the whip handle raised and lowered in his grasp, raised and lowered, circled in the grey air, and Tomlin knew that these little gestures could snap into action too swift for Tomlin to see, and the thong of ancient leather would snake out, *crack!* and curl fiercely on anything that threatened.

Tomlin, listening, decided the noises were echoes,

running around the shop. He faced the doorway to the back shop, and stepped one step towards it, and he knew the sounds were there, but he glanced at the rafters and the pale shapes watched him. Grandfather looked up; went to where the dust hung. 'Come down,' he said gently, and Tomlin gaped, and Pick crouched in fear, as the shapes moved, a face and hands, swinging down, small as Tomlin on to an island of shelves, lifted to the floor by Grandfather's whip hand; the knife held well away from her.

From the back shop silence listened.

'What's your name?' said Grandfather.

She retreated into a beam of sunlight, and her eyes stared. Hair tangled to her shoulders; her dress scarcely reached her legs. She was skinny and dirty, saw Tomlin, and Grandfather put his whip hand to his nose and sniffed.

'Tell me your name,' he said. 'Are you alone?' And shufflings hung in the air around the door to the back shop.

'I won't hurt you,' said Grandfather.

She moved her head as if seeking advice from someone unseen. She didn't speak, but light on her cheek showed Tomlin a bruise. He realized both her eyes were bruised, and her arm – as she lifted her hand towards the back shop – was pinched with more bruises.

'My name is Markham,' said Grandfather.

He waited, and silence listened again. 'This is Tomlin. And Pick.' Pause. 'We came looking for food. But we won't take any. It is yours. Markham,' he said again.

Her mouth opened.

'My name,' she said fearfully, 'is Yougirl.'

'Yougirl?'

A growl rumbled in Grandfather's throat, and the stock of the whip weaved urgent patterns in the air. He asked gently, 'Who calls you "Yougirl"?'

'Father,' she whispered. 'He is asleep. And Mother is asleep with the baby.' She gasped. Breath struggled in her nose. In the soft light a tear escaped rolling on the curve of her cheekbone, glittering on the bruise.

'Have you brothers and sisters?'

She sobbed, nodding towards the back shop, and the mutterings ceased, and feet came padding, children, among the shelves, slinking in shadows, beside the girl.

'Five,' whispered Grandfather.

'The baby is asleep. Mother said it would sleep. It was born with no mouth. They won't wake up.'

Grandfather stood very still. The whip hung loose in his hand. Then his head turned towards Tomlin, towards Pick. 'Do you understand?' he asked quietly, and Pick frowned, Tomlin opened his mouth and closed it again. Perhaps he understood. But Grandfather sighed and went into the back shop alone.

He came out and spat on the floor. Twice. Then he urged them towards the sunlight, saying, 'Come,' to the five children. Gently, 'Come. Come.' And they went, with Pick and Tomlin; bony arms dangling, fingers touching each other, hands shielding their faces from the light, weeping, murmuring, 'Outside! Outside!'

'Outside,' agreed Grandfather.

'We are forbidden!' whispered Yougirl. 'The Plant is wicked.'

'The Plant is wicked,' chorused the children.

Tomlin wondered at the words, wondered at the dirt and bruises on the thin limbs, insects in their hair.

'The Plant,' said Grandfather, 'is not wicked. Only people are wicked,' and his glance flared back towards the shop.

'Yougirl – ' Grandfather paused as three faces jerked up at him. Then he crouched, resting the knife, pulling the whip up in a curl around his shoulder. He reached for the smallest girl and she shrank fearfully. 'Tell me your name. I won't hurt you.'

'Yougirl,' she breathed.

Grandfather frowned and the five children stepped away. 'I won't hurt you,' he whispered, but he looked frightening, even to Tomlin, with the great knife at his feet and his mighty arm outstretched. Tomlin saw that the children had five fingers. 'Tell me,' whispered Grandfather to the third girl, 'tell me your name.'

'Yougirl.'

'And your brothers are both "Youboy"?' The two small boys gazed dumbly, bruises on white skin.

'Yes,' said the eldest girl.

'No,' said Grandfather. He stood up and offered his hand to her. She stared. 'Would you like a new name?' he said. 'A new name? I am Markham. Tomlin. Pick.' His arm swayed at Tomlin and Pick, then went back to her. 'Take my hand,' he told her, and she reached, cautiously, tips of her fingers touching his, ready to

71

snatch away, but Grandfather held her lightly. 'Will you come with us?' he asked.

She nodded.

'Will they follow?' Grandfather looked at the other children.

She nodded again.

'Come, then, and we will find you a new name. A new name for each of you.'

She hesitated, glancing into the shop.

'We will leave the baby,' murmured Grandfather, 'we will leave it to sleep.'

❧

They took the children through the Plant on the road, over the thick trunks to the roof, up and down the hot slates to the cut stumps, on to the sand.

Grandfather pointed at the stumps on the high tide mark. 'How long,' he asked, 'since we cut these?'

'The shadows have moved from here to here,' said Tomlin. He knelt, crying, 'It's growing!' for the stumps had shrivelled like wounds healing, and from the wounds, green sprouts curled.

'That's why,' said Grandfather, 'the Plant cannot simply be cut away. I wonder,' he whispered, 'how a stump would enjoy a drink of creosote?'

'Look.' Pick nodded towards the children.

They stood in a line, toes at the water, heads turning under the shelter of hands and forearms, reaching out to each other, reaching over the water as if to catch hold of something; backing, as Sequence sniffed knees; a little body bending closer to the boat, fingering the

72

rope, the smaller boy following the rope to the anchor and kneeling, breathing through his mouth, dumbfounded at the metal's sculptured shapes, pouncing with his five small fingers on a stone, dropping it for another; then one child jerking her foot when it touched the loch, crouching, patting fingertips on the water's surface; hands clutching sand, squeezing; faces to the sky; the other small boy risking dipping a foot, both feet; the first Yougirl finding seaweed, listening to it crackle, astonishment as bladders plopped under her step; and she turned, Yougirl, looking at Grandfather, and Grandfather smiled. Tomlin smiled. Pick smiled.

Yougirl came to Grandfather.

She stood not quite touching him. She stared at Tomlin; and edged closer to Grandfather, watching his face, beginning to lean on him.

'Child,' said Grandfather, 'we won't hurt you.' And she wept again, a great weeping, letting herself relax in Grandfather's embrace. And the smallest boy at the anchor wept, and Tomlin, not sure what to do, knelt with him; then Tomlin smiled, for the others began, whimpering, howling, all gathering around Grandfather and Pick, strong arms gathering them, voices rolling thinly across the water.

Then they were calm, and Grandfather said they must get into the boat, and Tomlin was amazed, for the children did not understand.

'Don't you know what a boat is?' he cried, and heads shook.

'We're not allowed outside,' said the eldest girl.

'Never?'

73

'Never.'

A sigh from Grandfather that seemed to rumble, threatening as thunder, around the hills. Then he handed Tomlin the knife, and with the whip still curled on his shoulder, lifted two children and waded, rather unsteadily, chest deep to the boat which bobbed high on the tide.

Pick followed, carrying another two, mouth tight against lapping water, then he returned for the last little girl.

'You can't swim with that,' he told Tomlin, and held out his hand for the knife.

He waited, his good eye warm, without cunning.

Grandfather, dripping in the boat, watched, and Tomlin passed the knife to Pick and stepped back.

Pick grinned, his pea eye bobbing. 'Markham,' he said. 'Not Aunt Bolliter.' And he strode into the loch carrying the child and the glittering blade; and Tomlin grasped the anchor, waiting for the rope to slacken as the tide lifted the yacht – then heaved the fluke out of the sand, and ran as the anchor dragged through sea-weed down the beach, and swam, pushing Sequence, the water warm, Tomlin showing off a little to the row of fists and faces at the yacht's rail, swimming under-water, rising close to the boat, adding his fists to the rail, grinning, saying, 'Ha!' into a pair of startled eyes, heaving the dog into the children's arms; and glimpsing Grandfather's smile, Tomlin turned deep, hauling with his palms against the water, struggling down the descending curve of the hull, under the keel, stones rubbing his feet, thrusting against the stones and up the other side bursting! into sunlight, gasping, 'Hah!' laughing as the heads turned in astonishment. Then he pulled himself on board, and it seemed right that he should touch Yougirl's face with his wet hands.

'Can we sail?' asked Tomlin.

'Can you whistle up a wind?' cried Grandfather, as he hauled the anchor on board. So Tomlin whistled as Grandfather stowed the anchor and showed Pick how to wedge it; he whistled an old tune, and the children stared. 'It's called Happy Birthday To You,' explained Tomlin, 'but it doesn't mean anything.' So he whistled and pointed and the children stared again, as the water at the head of the loch flattened suddenly, then rippled, the ripples rushing south as wind poured off the hills.

'Well done, Mister Mate!' cried Grandfather. 'Let's have the boat trim! Clear the boom, there, me hearties!' And Tomlin urged the startled children to sit here and here and over there, to balance the yacht, and in no time Grandfather's fingers had unfurled the sail, hoisted it, and sent it billowing, tugging the mast, catching the pushing air, and the little boat ceased its wandering – wandering since the anchor was raised – dipped once towards the shore, then slid away; heads turning rapidly, watching Tomlin ease the tiller, chins up to glimpse the beach shrinking behind them, eyes down to the ruffled water pouring past the hull, unfolding into thin, long waves that followed each other, some to the shore, others rolling across the loch.

In seconds the pier swept past and the whole wonderful stretch of water glittered and rippled this way and that, turning dark, brightening, and Tomlin laughed at the wonder on the children's faces, and Grandfather sang Happy Birthday To You in a voice that mingled with the breeze, then hesitated, as he faced Yougirl, searching for a name. Then he glanced at Tomlin. 'Your mother's name?' he asked. 'Shall we give her your mother's name?' And Tomlin nodded eagerly. 'Happy birthday, dear Patricia,' sang Grandfather, 'happy birthday to you!'

'Patricia?' said Patricia. Her bruised face experimented with a smile.

'Patricia!' cried Tomlin.

'Keep her steady, Mister Mate!' yelled Grandfather as he ducked into the cabin and reappeared with the bag of potato cakes. Tomlin beamed for he was very hungry, but Grandfather's eye pinned his mouth shut. And the potato cakes went to the children, who never ceased staring, and it was Patricia who bit first, and the others watched, then teeth tore and the cakes vanished, fingers licked until more cakes appeared and disappeared.

'I left the waterbottle,' said Grandfather regretfully. 'But we'll be home soon.' And the breeze drew a tear from his eye. 'Mister Mate,' he said, turning his back on the crew, 'give the tiller to Pick.'

'Yes, Grandfather.' Tomlin changed places with the Poor Soul, and held Grandfather's hand.

'You'll have to jump ashore and put a line round the bollard.'

'Aye, Cap'n,' said Tomlin. 'They'll need a wash, Grandfather. The little one's scratching bugs all over the boat.'

Grandfather laughed, and they enjoyed the sail into the broad waters of the estuary. Pick steered towards the island; avoiding the mast of the sunken yacht. Opposite the greenhouse Grandfather dropped the sail. Tomlin stood at the bow conscious of five astonished pairs of eyes; the stern line light in his grasp. The greenhouse slid past.

'A little closer to shore,' ordered Grandfather. Water flopped between the hull and the rocks, slapping, swaying the boat, the shore slipping past; the first cement stump approaching.

Tomlin jumped. Little voices cried out. He hitched the rope to the bollard as the yacht moved past, rocking more with the thrust of Tomlin's leap; he held the rope, letting it slide around the bollard, slowing the yacht; stopping it; securing the rope; catching another attached to the bow, hitching it tight to the second stump, kicking tyres – tied to the stumps – to dangle between the boat and rocks.

'Well done!' cried Grandfather. 'All ashore, me hearties!' And he and Pick lifted the children, and they stood on the grass, eyes round, gazing at the house with its water tank on top, the greenhouse mirroring the sun, the soft ranks of vegetables, and trees drooping with unripe fruit; the pulley rope reaching from the north shore, descending south; the town –

'Now,' said Grandfather. He put Sequence on the grass, and waited until Pick landed with the knife and plastic bag. 'You are going to learn to swim! Mister Mate!'

'Aye, Cap'n!'

'Dive!'

'Aye, aye, Cap'n!'

'And while you're about it – '

Tomlin ran down the slope of the shore and dived, and as his fingers divided the water he heard, ' – close the dam!' then the water exploded around his head, and he was down, below the dappling surface, pushing hard with frog strokes of his legs, hauling through the cool depths with his palms. Then up he popped, half-blinded by glitter, and swam into the boathouse; he climbed up to the floor that was a shelf, and wound a handle to the whirring of chains; fast he wound and from the rafters descended a wall of wood, the bottom edge curved, and the curve struck the water and sank, and the top edge appeared and stopped above the water's surface. The dam blocked the basin that normally held the boat.

'Ready!' yelled Tomlin, and his voice screamed, like a boy in a bottle, between the walls and water, and the children came, silent and full of wonder at the noisy slopping, the bouncing light.

'They'll drown in here!' cried Tomlin.

'Here comes the spoon!' roared Grandfather, who was fond of his cleverness with pulleys, and he wound two handles at once, then let Pick wind one, and from the dappled darkness creaked the spoon, but such a spoon! gasps from five mouths, down it crept, as long as Grandfather, its giant handle scooped out like a chute, bump, resting across the dam, splash! as the spoon's bowl struck the water, rocking like a boat. And Tomlin leaned on the bowl, sinking it, the handle still on the dam; then chains whirred and the bowl rose, full, its water pouring along the chute and into the loch.

'Again!' cried Grandfather.

'Again!' whispered Patricia.

'Again!' echoed timid voices, and again the spoon dipped and poured water from the boathouse into the loch; and again and again until the water wobbled around Tomlin's knees.

'Ready, I think!' said Tomlin.

'Out y'come!' cried Grandfather. 'In you go!' he encouraged the children. 'In you go, my lovelies! Come.' But they stood against the wall. He took Patricia by the hands and she slid down to the water, where she faced her brothers and sisters on the shelf. She faced Grandfather and Tomlin and Pick. She looked at the water plopping at her knees, patted it suddenly banging her palms on the surface, smiling the tiniest smile, widening her smile for Grandfather, nodding, reaching up for her smallest sister; and in a minute they were all in the water, and Grandfather asked Tomlin to fetch soap, and when he returned, stepping around the door of the boathouse, shrieks of laughter rang across the estuary, and Tomlin gaped as clothing drifted out and swirled away in the current.

Grandfather and Pick stood shin deep beside the children, persuading the middle girl to part with her dress. Tomlin threw in soap and Grandfather told him he must find something clean for his new family to wear – and bring a comb!

So he ran again under the late sun, and remembered the bees. He walked on the bridge, bees bumbling past him, yellow legged with pollen. On the grass he stood, and said, 'We're back. Thank you for looking after the island. Grandfather and Pick and me, we're back. Pick is on our side now, I think. And we've brought others. Smaller than me. They are our new family. They are intelligent like Grandfather, with five fingers. I'll introduce them to you later. They're getting washed. Thank you. Buzz.' And not a bee touched his skin, but the bees' song thickened in the air as he spoke, then faded, and Tomlin thanked them again and ran to the house; meeting Sequence who stood gasping on the metal path. 'Water?' cried Tomlin, and Sequence walked as Tomlin ran to splash water into a dish, and the old dog lapped noisily, eyeing the fish that dropped beside the water.

Then Tomlin hunted through the three caravans, half-thinking about bed space, as he gathered garments and maybe-garments; rushed past Sequence and the chewed fish; remembered the comb; dashed inside, stuck the comb in his hair, ran bundled high, trailing a shirt, tripping, staggering, gasping, laughing, dancing around the shirt's sleeve, hopping and trotting on to the grass by the boathouse; and laughing more as five naked bodies under hair as tangled-wet as seaweed, rushed round from the boathouse door, shrieking and giggling on to the grass, the middle girl slightly tearful, thought Tomlin, into the sunshine.

And Tomlin stopped laughing, seeing their bony legs and bruised white skin. Then he threw the clothes here and there about the grass, keeping his best shirt for Patricia. And they pulled the clothes on, making Pick and Grandfather laugh, for only Patricia's shirt fitted, the other children quite drowned, quite up-to-their-ears and down-to-the-ground; the smallest boy grand as an emperor in a storybook, wrapped in a robe of red, white and blue – a Union Jack.

Then the comb went chug-chugging down heads, with many 'Ohs!' and more tears, and much careful wiping of the comb, and Grandfather saying he would make a finer comb to strip their hair really clean, and he brightened tear-damp faces by cutting off tangled hair, dropping it on to the loch, waving goodbye as it spun south in the slow swirl of the tide.

And then they ate; Pick and Patricia and four little ones, sitting at the north window, Sequence a snoring cushion for naked feet, Tomlin and Grandfather busy at the gas, boiling carrots, potatoes and broad beans, frying fish sprinkled with salt and parsley, wishing for an extra frying pan – more fish frizzling, water to drink, flavoured with honey and fruit juice; apples from a shelf in one of Grandfather's garden sheds. And suddenly, two children slept at the table, and Tomlin put down the double bed in the middle caravan, and children – slung over Grandfather's shoulder, others staggering with sleep – were bundled into bed, a bundle of five, still in their clothes, the smallest still inside his Union Jack, a single sheet over them.

Tomlin went to his bed, opening the window wide, kneeling, watching the sun roll low along the northern hills; go below the hills leaving the sky silver and pink, and he heard the hose rattling on the standpipe and knew Grandfather was watering the crops. Then he lay down picturing the children through the wall, seeing them laughing and eating; and he woke from a doze at the tread of Pick's feet on the veranda and Grandfather's voice – for no one ever heard Grandfather's feet – and Tomlin half-opened his eyes, sighing, seeing the midnight luminance of the sun below the hills, hearing Pick say he could not go back, and Grandfather agreeing that he should sleep in the greenhouse.

Tomlin woke to the smell of burning. He sat up. The night beyond his open window was a gloaming of silver water and black hills. The smell was Grandfather's tobacco.

Tomlin rose, padding through the middle caravan, where the bundle of children breathed and sighed; found Grandfather in his armchair at the north window.

The tantalus stood open on the table, its silver lock a blot in the dusk. A red spot glowed as Grandfather sucked a cigar.

'Hah,' said Grandfather quietly. 'Have a cigar, old man.'

Tomlin chose an imaginary cigar from Grandfather's tin, struck a silent match and puffed smoke that set him coughing – but not noisily enough to waken the children.

'Well,' said Grandfather.

Grandfather's eyes moved in the gloom, looking around cheerfully. 'Our house has shrunk,' he murmured, nodding towards the middle caravan. 'Kind of you to give them my bed.'

'There's a bed here, old man,' said Tomlin patting the

seat and ignoring Grandfather's crinkling eye. 'Is Pick staying with us?'

'Can't send him back.'

'He can't stay in the greenhouse. Winter – '

'How d'you fancy – '

'What?'

'Well. Moving. Moving away. There'll be trouble, you know. Margrit.' Grandfather sighed through his cigar. 'She sent Pick to kill us,' he whispered lightly, 'but all Pick needed was someone to talk sense to him. Imagine having no company but that mad woman and the Poor Souls . . . I don't think he's a Poor Soul.'

'Are the children . . . ?'

'Oh, they're not! They are not! Won't that be trouble! When she finds out that not just you and your old Grandad are cleverer than she is! but five others! All normal! Think on her anger! You and me dead now, she hopes! then five more! Ho! She will be madder than she ever was! Hmn.'

In the silence of the night a whimper drifted through the open windows, but it wasn't repeated, and Grandfather sipped the headmaster's brandy and Tomlin drew on his cigar. He thought of the awful mountainous Bolliter and two pairs of spectacles around those dead-fish eyes, and moved his shoulders uncomfortably.

'Where would we go, Grandfather? Is the Plant not all over the world?'

'It may be,' whispered Grandfather behind the glow of his cigar. 'But the town is not covered. And we found those children even where the Plant had come. Perhaps there are others. And if we find others . . .'

'What?'

'What? Oh. I don't know. Maybe, if we find enough, and creosote will kill the Plant. If. It would require many people. Would you mind? Would it bother you to leave this place?'

'No,' breathed Tomlin. 'Not with you.'

'And the children?'

'Mm.'

'And Pick?'

'I don't mind Pick.'

'Maybe we would come back here. Rebuild the town. Or one of the islands in the estuary – '

'A real island?'

'A real island. Clear the Plant away. Farm the land. If creosote works . . .'

Tomlin yawned and blinked.

'Put your cigar out carefully,' chuckled Grandfather.

'Goodnight, Grandfather.'

'Goodnight. You're the best boy.' Tomlin hugged his Grandfather and a five-fingered hand rubbed his hair.

'Sleep well.'

'Goodnight, old man,' yawned Tomlin, and went in search of his bed. And the island hummed a lullaby, rocking him to sleep.

'Hold it like this, Jack,' said Grandfather to the smallest boy. And the island shimmered with laughter as tiny wrists flicked the fishing rod and the Union Jack descended round his ankles.

84

'Haw! Haw! Haw!' roared Grandfather. 'Perhaps we'd better wait till y'r old Grandad stitches together a pair of trousers! Haw! Haw! Haw! Haw!'

Patricia giggled close to Tomlin's shoulder. Tomlin thought her legs looked fatter already, and the bruises less on her white skin. With the sun promising more heat, her skin would be red today and brown tomorrow. Her eyes, he saw, sparkled behind the wonder. Already her fear was gone.

Then she stared, forgetting the laughter, and Tomlin turned to discover what she saw in the town.

'Oh,' he said. 'Grandfather!'

And Grandfather paused as he folded and tied the Union Jack into a skirt around the smallest boy. 'I see,' he said to Tomlin. 'I hope it stays up.' Jack beamed at Grandfather and Grandfather stood. He glanced at Pick and Pick stared towards the town.

A group of people moved through the weeds on the shore road. They came slowly, staggering, Margrit Bolliter sunk in a chair, the chair held up by Poor Souls; wending a path around trees; the mad woman, saw Tomlin, eating.

Patricia's fingers crept inside Tomlin's arm. The other children moved away from the fishing rods and stood close to Grandfather. Even at this distance, the black wig sat tilted, and the spectacles made a strange mask.

'Don't worry,' said Grandfather. 'Don't be afraid, Tomlin.'

Tomlin looked at Grandfather, and Grandfather's face was grim and slightly sad. His blue gaze withdrew from the town and he smiled at Tomlin and inclined his head towards the house.

'Yes, Grandad!' said Tomlin. He caught Patricia's fingers. 'Come on!' She ran with him, among the bushy leaves of potatoes; between the dry claws of apple and plum trees, through the rows of onions and carrots, into the house, making Sequence raise his head from shade in the doorway where he already hid from the sun.

Tomlin opened a cupboard and lifted the whip from its hook. He uncoiled it, flicking it gently, letting it wriggle the length of the caravan.

'He had it with him,' whispered Patricia, 'on the boat. What is it?'

'You'll see,' said Tomlin. 'Maybe. Grandfather doesn't like to use it. Come on!'

Out he ran, on to the veranda, Patricia following, her fingers finding his hand, Sequence pushing past his ankles.

Grandfather strode among the fruit trees, his white hair thick and wild, children trotting, touching each other, little Jack in the red, white and blue skirt, holding Pick's hand; like elfin children, thought Tomlin, startled by sunlight.

Grandfather's fingers took the whip, and Tomlin, with Patricia, ran beside him. Sequence flolloped down the veranda steps, standing straight on his woolly legs, full of curiosity. 'Come!' urged Tomlin, and the dog caught up when they stopped behind Grandfather at the bridge.

The chair, with Margrit Bolliter eating on it, still

approached among the trees of the shore road. Past the monument.

Someone stumbled, and across the beach Bolliter's voice raged. Then on they came, six Poor Souls, counted Tomlin, carrying the awful woman bloated with fat.

'Stop!' Tomlin heard the clucking of the bell in her palm. The Poor Souls lowered the chair; beyond the beehives and the dry lawn. The water of the estuary swirled suckingly between the lawn and the island. Bees swung in their wandering flight, across the bridge. The sun stretched its arms and beamed on the children and Margrit Bolliter.

Two Poor Souls – one was Rem with the white hair – helped Margrit to stand. She thrust them away and approached the lawn, stumping *this-leg that-leg*; her sack-of-flour neck swaying, her two pairs of spectacles like a spider clinging on her eyes.

She stood on the lawn.

'Angry old woman,' murmured Grandfather, and Tomlin glanced at Grandfather then at Bolliter, and remembered she was a survivor of the war. He hadn't thought of her as old. But she was angry. Her face shone white beneath the black wig. Her huge arms quivered.

'Pick!'

Her voice was sharp but low. She tried a smile.

'Come back. Pick! You didn't come back! You didn't –'

She stopped talking, as if realizing her words would give something away.

'You didn't kill us,' said Grandfather to Pick, and Pick swayed with embarrassment.

The whip hung lightly in Grandfather's right hand.

Bolliter's head went up and down, silently.

'She's avoiding the beehives,' said Tomlin, as she moved across the lawn, balancing in her neat shoes to where the lawn joined the beach and sat on the grass, gasp! fat on her arms wobbling, fat on her neck swinging, wig slipping, horribly determined, easing down the little slope to the beach, crunching on sea-weed, bending and panting, but unable to reach down to the stones, and she wheezed, 'Renton! Here! Here!' And a thin man went to her, and gave her stones, and she hurled one viciously, diamonds flashing, towards the island.

Renton waved away a bee.

The children moved nervously, but the stone sped at an angle and struck the caravan, spilling petals as it passed among the azaleas.

'Get behind the house,' ordered Grandfather. 'Take Sequence.' And Tomlin hurried the children, lifting Jack, running, calling the dog. A stone struck the bridge.

Tomlin returned to Grandfather and Pick, and thought that Grandfather's eyes glanced kindly on him for a moment; then Grandfather called out.

'Can't fool you, Margrit!' he said.

The grotesque figure paused, arm raised, wig at a different angle.

'You sent us for tins,' said Grandfather, 'and we brought children.'

The arm lowered. Margrit Bolliter's mouth opened, but she stared, searching for Renton's wrist, leaning on him.

'She's so furious,' murmured Grandfather, 'that she hardly saw them. She knows now. I wouldn't kill the bees!' called Grandfather as Renton's free arm beat the air.

'Children!' hissed Bolliter. Her enormous chest rose and fell as she breathed. 'Children!' Her hands turned into fists, and she swung backwards a blow that knocked Renton on to the rocks. The fists quivered. Her head quivered. Her lips twitched, and Tomlin watched horrified, as froth bubbled on to her chin, and the fat mass of her body juddered rigidly, and she stood very straight, then fell back, stiff as stone, her head striking Renton, and the neat feet drummed on the beach insanely.

'Come!' said Grandfather. 'Come!' he ordered, as Pick hesitated. And he ran, shouting at the Poor Souls on the road to bring the chair, and they shuffled, raising the chair, Nancy – Tomlin saw – being shaken by one of the Poor Souls, to make her move.

They crossed the lawn and sat the chair on the rocks beside Margrit Bolliter, and as the fat woman lay struggling, her fit ended; they lifted her, bald head glinting, into the chair and she shrieked foully until Grandfather threw the wig into her lap, and he ordered them away, cracking the whip, talking loudly and harshly to drown the demented woman's instructions, and the Poor Souls staggered to the road and Grandfather drove them on, the whip ripping the air around their ears, his voice bellowing, rolling between the beach and the distant islands.

◆

Grandfather's wicked little fish knife split another fish belly, guts in the bucket, wash; Tomlin sizzling fish in fish-oil in the frying pan, slices of potato browning nicely, dried seaweed sprinkled on for colour and piquancy. 'She's thinking!' growled Grandfather, *slit!* wash. 'Thinking. Slowly. Slowly!' *Slit!* guts-in-the-bucket. 'But she's thinking! Bolliter. What's she going t'do, boy? I don't know.' *Slit.* 'But her rage is endless. She's a dangerous woman. Like the fool who pushed the button. Too much emotion, too much power; not enough control.' He cut the last fish. 'Enough?'

'Yes, Grandfather.'

'I'll call them in,' said Grandfather, and he splashed water around the sink, cleaning it of blood and bones and fish scales. 'Sure you've enough? Smells great. Y'r a good boy.'

He went into the mid-morning sun, and Tomlin eased the last fish in the pan to prevent it burning, decided it was cooked; turned off the gas, and dashed plates, hot from the oven, busily-full of fish and potatoes, to the table, and in they came, Pick and children, Grandfather; beaming, giggling, touching, shaking wet hair, well combed into strands and shadows; clothes sticking to half-dry bodies.

'They'd be cleaner!' laughed Grandfather, 'if the soap would lather in the salt water. Haw! Ah! Look at that breakfast!'

A rush of half-dry bodies around the table. 'Start eating!' yelled Tomlin. 'Did your skirt stay up, Jack?'

Jack nodded at Tomlin, then put fork and fingers to his potato. He sucked his fingers, scowling.

'It's hot,' warned Tomlin.

'Union Jack!' said Jack.

'Yes – '

'Union Jack!' roared Grandfather. 'Another clever one! Eat up! Eat up!'

'Union Jack outside. Union Jack up.'

'The Union Jack is round your tummy,' said Tomlin, enjoying his fish, and he smiled at Grandfather and looked at the children, glad they were eating his food, glad they were his family.

'Union Jack outside. Union Jack up.' Little Jack's face beamed at Tomlin and his tiny five fingers pointed at the caravan's roof.

'It's there!' laughed Tomlin, tugging Jack's skirt.

Grandfather rose suddenly and went out. He returned, grimly. He smiled. 'Eat up, my lovelies! Tomlin,' he said firmly, 'eat up quickly.'

Tomlin stared at Grandfather for a moment. Grandfather nodded at Tomlin's plate, and Tomlin ate swiftly, drank honeyed water, followed Grandfather outside.

'Look.'

Across the glimmering water, beyond the church spire, just below a window in a block of brick-red flats, a Union Jack hung.

'The life-or-death signal!' gasped Tomlin. 'We must hurry!'

But Grandfather looked around, gazing across the

estuary, smiling a little at the seagull rending fish guts on the grass. His eye followed the length of the pulley rope; he blinked up at the sun; gazed down at Tomlin.

'Perhaps,' he said. 'Perhaps . . .'

'But it's the signal!'

'Maybe.'

'Maybe!'

Grandfather's eye crinkled thoughtfully. Sequence came down the veranda steps and sat at Grandfather's feet. The sun laid a hot palm on Tomlin's cheek.

'She is very angry,' said Grandfather. 'Very, very angry. More angry, in fact, than you and I can understand.'

'But the flag – !'

'Don't you see!' said Grandfather, and Sequence looked up. 'It may not be a life-or-death signal. Just death. For me. Then afterwards – ' He turned his hand towards the caravan where the children devoured fish and potato garnished with seaweed.

'We must go,' said Tomlin firmly.

'Don't you see – ?'

'We must go. Grandfather – ' Tomlin looked at Grandfather severely. 'Someone may be hurt.'

Grandfather's blue gaze drifted on to Tomlin and hung over him. Tomlin waited. Grandfather's head nodded gently and a smile grew. 'Right as usual,' he said. 'Bring the first-aid box.'

Tomlin smiled at his grandfather because he loved him; then ran. He returned, wearing socks and shoes, with the box and the whip. Pick came, with Patricia behind him.

'The Union Jack is showing.' Grandfather pointed, and Pick frowned. 'Tomlin says we must go.'

'I will come,' said Pick.

'You must look after the children,' said Grandfather.

Tomlin held Patricia's hand, then followed Grandfather towards the bridge.

Grandfather said, 'Stay,' to Sequence, and the old dog sat in the shade by the bridge's wheels. Grandfather stood before the beehives, bees gathering on his face until he was bearded with their living fur. 'Look after the children.' Bees on his lips forced him to whisper. 'And Pick. Protect the island. If I don't return –' Bees rose with an angry buzzing, more and more pouring from the hives. 'Pick and the children are yours. Keep them safe. We must go to Margrit Bolliter.' And bee by bee, Grandfather's whiskers lessened and went droning into the sunlight.

Grandfather walked swiftly, the whip tight in his right hand. Tomlin looked back, and saw Sequence trotting on the bridge, stopping, gathering his bottom under him, sitting. Tomlin waved, and hurried through the weeds, the first-aid box swinging by its handle from his three fingers.

Grandfather slowed. He sighed, striding lightly, the whip alive in his grasp, eyes alert. 'I don't like it,' he said. 'She hasn't had time to think anything up. She used to be normal, y'know. Swimming. Winning cups.'

'Yes, Grandfather.'

'The war changed her.'

'Yes.'

'But there's still some intelligence!'

'Grandfather.'

'What? What. Am I going on? I hate this!' He stopped, looking across the sunny water. 'Why! Why does she need to be best! If she could accept herself for what she is – What's the point in striving to be better than anyone else! There's always someone better at something.' He looked down at Tomlin. 'But there's no one better at being you, than yourself. Competition, boy; competition as a principle is foolish. Wickedly foolish!' His whip hand gestured at the Plant on the islands. He opened his mouth; but merely breathed a long, 'Oh'.

Then he walked slowly, grass crackling, insects floating through the weeds, the river a drifting glitter, 'bright as Bolliter's knuckles' rumbled Grandfather.

A distant bark made them turn. Sequence sat looking through the rail of the bridge.

'Come on,' sighed Grandfather. 'Let's get it over. It's so foolish.'

＊

They passed the monument, then the putting green. They approached the church and the tall buildings. Shadows always lay between these two, thought Tomlin. His legs itched under the stocking rims. Rising pollen made him sneeze and he *tissued!* laughing, curling forward *tissue!* seeing Grandfather striding through the shadow *tissue!* following the path of crushed vegetation; Tomlin pausing *tissue!* noticing grass and white umbrellas of saxifrage broken between the path and church door, and he remembered the worn floor in the shop, and *tissue – !*

'Come on,' said Grandfather.

Tomlin ran.

'All right?'

'Good sneeze!' said Tomlin.

'There it is,' said Grandfather, as if he regretted going to the red-brick flats. 'Plenty of birds.'

They stepped slowly between the rhododendrons, and the large flowers – pink and red – were open mouths for bees to drink at.

Grandfather pointed at the flattened ground. 'That's where the Poor Souls rested her chair. They carry it on a door with poles nailed along it as handles.' He gazed up, searching the sagging roof above the door.

Sycamores and pink weeds sprouted, still and silent, groaning almost, thought Tomlin, at the rising heat of the sun.

'Nothing to fall on us,' said Grandfather.

'Grandfather, it may be a real signal for help.'

'Hmm.' Grandfather waved the whip. 'Then why is there no one here to hurry us up the stairs? That would only be natural! Markham is coming! Go and meet him! Show him where the accident is! Nothing. Nobody. Let's go! Let's get it over!'

They went into the hall among the bin bags, then backed out into the fresh air.

'What a stench!'

'Oooh!' groaned Tomlin. 'Maybe you're right, Grandfather. She's trying to poison us!'

'A quick dash,' said Grandfather, and they ran, holding breaths, through the hall, up the stairs, open-the-door-shut-the-door! *Gasp!*

95

'Oh, no!' cried Tomlin. 'It's almost as bad! Why would she do that!'

The carpet path on the polished lino was strewn with garbage. Black sacks, bobbing with flies, stood in crowds; in corners, around Bolliter's gold door.

'But she keeps it so clean!' cried Tomlin.

Grandfather strode to the brass knocker, and thundered metallically. 'It's just been done!' growled Grandfather glancing at the clean ƎMOϽ⅃ƎW mat. 'Ha. The door's open.'

He pushed it wide, that gold door. Daylight stood among Bolliter's shining furniture and dumbly pointing clocks. Grandfather went in cautiously. 'Anyone there? That smell. There's something different,' he whispered over his shoulder. 'An old smell. Familiar. Oh, familiar! I know it! But it's slight, and all that stench.' Tomlin shut the door.

They entered the living room, with the paintings hanging from the ceiling occupying Grandfather's headroom. He looked through other doorways.

'We'd better go.'

Tomlin opened the window to let the smell out.

'Grandfather. Why would she do that?'

'What has she done? Fence posts?'

Fence posts.

Hammered into the ground. A little forest of sticks pointing up.

'So we can't jump out!' growled Grandfather. 'Come on! Run!'

But as they turned from the window, a strange rushing sound rose from below, as if a wind had been trapped in the hallway and stairs. Glass crashed, and the sound wooshed closer beyond the door of Aunt Bolliter's apartment. Something boomed, and Tomlin pointed along the little hall. Smoke wisped in through the keyhole and feathered under the door.

Grandfather leaned out the window. Tomlin squeezed beside him. Flames struggled from the shattered hall window below.

'And we can't jump!' hissed Grandfather.

'Grandfather. What can we do?'

'Well, we can't go down the stairs. Solid fire all the way. Did y'hear the petrol can exploding? Run to the other windows! Quick! Now – ' said Grandfather as Tomlin returned shaking his head.

'More fence posts, Grandfather.'

' – that door is half-hour fireproof. Or used to be. Let's see. The floor. The ceiling. No point in going up . . . Right. Into the kitchen! Close the door!'

He opened a drawer. 'Hold the whip, old chap.' He used a bread knife to dig into the pink-papered wall. 'Plaster-board,' he said. 'Then a bit of soundproofing. Then more plasterboard. All I have to do is clear the edge – '

He stopped working and stared round at Tomlin. The look in Grandfather's eyes made Tomlin step back. 'We don't have half-an-hour!' whispered Grandfather. 'She has destroyed her world – ' The tilt of his jaw indicated the building they were in, ' – just to kill me. So where is she now? She's dodged us somewhere. She's going to the island! The children! The children!' he roared. And Tomlin staggered back against a cooker, his eyes wide, heart drumming at the fearful twisting of Grandfather's

97

face; and the knife swung high as though it would descend through Tomlin's body, but Grandfather turned his back on Tomlin, and from his rising fist the knife flew to clatter into Bolliter's sink; but the fist continued to rise, closed itself tight, knuckles a bundle of rock, then descended towards the wall; and Grandfather's magnificent body spun on the ball of his left foot and the mighty arm, with all the energy of a supreme physical being, slammed against the wallpaper; denting it; the plasterboard under the paper burst, dust exploding whitely, gaping darkness; Grandfather's arm vanished into the hole, up to his elbow.

Then both his hands were ripping away the plasterboard, and in seconds Tomlin was coughing white dust and Grandfather was stepping into the next-door apartment.

Tomlin followed, awkward with the whip and first-aid box. Grandfather had the outer door opened.

Tomlin ran.

Grandfather had gone. Tomlin followed the sound of something splintering. Along a carpet path he ran. Dust and debris undisturbed for a generation. Down a flight of steps. Doors with names. Names for tombstones.

Bright daylight. Tomlin ran over a door that lay flat on weeds, fresh splinters around the lock and hinges.

He ran through a crushed path towards the shore-end of the building, away from the fire. Smoke rolled black into the sky. He ran in the shadow of the smoke. He ran fiercely knowing Grandfather was ahead breaking desperately through untrodden vegetation.

Tomlin rejoined the usual path close to the church.

Grandfather was running among the trees on the shore road. He was already past the putting green and the monument.

Tomlin raced on, panting hard, sweat on his face. He glanced back. Smoke towered in an awful black column, and the sun floated behind it, like the moon behind clouds.

Terrible crashes followed Tomlin. He fled. Grandfather had stopped before reaching the beehives.

The Poor Souls, with Margrit Bolliter, had just arrived, saw Tomlin. For Grandfather was urging the Poor Souls away from the hives, and his voice was raised in reasonableness to the mad woman who stood between the hives and the bridge. She screamed words that Tomlin couldn't catch, and he heard Grandfather say 'bees' over and over, trying to project sense through the woman's insane ragings.

Her left hand flapped the air, slapped her own skin. Her right hand, Tomlin saw as he ran close, held a brick.

'Margrit, the bees!' cried Grandfather. 'Come away – !'

But she backed towards the bridge, the brick raised warningly. The bees' song increased. She slapped at her thighs, and hurled the brick at a beehive.

'No – !' gasped Grandfather.

She turned, mountainous in a yellow summer dress, black wig a-glitter, fingers bright with diamonds, stumping, *running* on mammoth legs on to the bridge. The flesh of her arms grew brown with bees. She brushed bees off. She thudded, the bridge shaking under her weight. Bees swarmed on her back and legs. She paused to wipe her calves but the fur gathered again. She staggered a few paces, off the bridge on to the island. Sequence barked.

Grandfather yelled at Pick and the children to stay away. The bees would not recognize friends in time of war.

Bolliter stood on the grass above the slope of Grandfather's rock and cement shore. She twisted every way, slapping, wiping; bees fell. Scores stung, and died in flight. She wiped both hands down her face, losing her pairs of spectacles, sobbing, wailing in rage, flailing herself; she stumbled to her hands and knees; her wig plopped off and rolled on the grass. She reached for it, blindly. Bees gathered on her bald head. Every bit of flesh that Tomlin saw as she brushed the living fur away was violently red with stings. She reached again for the wig and her hand went down the slope of the shore and she rolled over the rocks but couldn't hold on for the need to beat her own flesh. She slid into the water, and a thousand bees drowned. Others rose around her, their song a song of fury and victory.

She floated. Bolliter, Margrit Bolliter, floated on her back, buoyant with fat. Then she turned face down and swam, her bald dome dipping, then rising red, dipping . . .

She relaxed, and slowly rolled on to her back, one massive arm limp across her stomach. The arm dropped into the water; bees floated, struggling. Bolliter floated, quietly. Her yellow dress, bright as sunshine, her flesh red with bee stings; and the current flowing under the bridge, squeezing between the island and the lawn, turned the body this way, then that; then seemed to decide that headfirst was easiest, and floated her downstream, bobbing, diamonds sparkling; and in a minute the woman was a yellow blob rising and dipping far beyond the south shore; beyond the nodding fishing rods.

Tomlin found he was kneeling on the grass, staring along the water's bright surface. On the island the children and Pick approached the shore. Patricia was crying.

The taste of smoke reached Tomlin. He stood up holding the first-aid box. He handed the whip to Grandfather.

'Rem,' said Grandfather. The white-haired man approached avoiding the beehives, coughing slightly.

'Where are the other Poor Souls?' cried Tomlin.

'Run off,' said Grandfather. 'Or wandered off. We'd better move!' He caught Tomlin's wrist, and ran ordering Rem to follow, and they crossed the bridge, avoiding bees in the air, crushing bees underfoot.

A breeze trickled on Tomlin's skin.

'The fire's creating its own draught!' said Grandfather. They stood with the children. Pick spoke reassuringly to Rem. Smoke towered higher than the sun, and fire lit the shadows between the church and the tall buildings. Smoke wisped from several parts of the spire's wooden surface. From the shadows a wall of crackling flame advanced along the shore road.

The breeze pressed Tomlin's back. The mass of smoke poured away for a moment; on the spire, flames gnawed savagely, rising triumphantly, until the church burned like a giant matchstick. With a terrible sound the high structure fell, folding on to the body of the church, revealing, beyond, the half-eaten remains of the red-brick flats.

Then the wind changed and smoke closed down on the whole terrible scene, and the wall of flame advanced along the shore road. The roar of roasting air was dreadful, and Patricia clung to Tomlin as the fire began to run, fast as a man, over the putting green.

'There's nothing left for us here!' shouted Grandfather.

Tomlin looked up at him, then reached to Grandfather's hair and removed a red petal. White dust from the wall of Bolliter's kitchen stuck to the sweat of Grandfather's face; powdered his shirt.

'We haven't much time,' said Grandfather quietly. And Tomlin knew what Grandfather was about to say, and he let his mouth fall open.

'We must.' Grandfather's hand clasped Tomlin's shoulder. 'The smoke will kill us. Fetch the hammer, there's a good lad. Hurry. Hurry, my boy.'

Tomlin walked. Patricia's hands trailed off his arm. Then he darted to a garden hut. For a moment, the dimness baffled his eyes, then he laid hold of a hammer as long as himself, and stepped into sunlight.

'This way!' Grandfather was hastening to the south shore.

Tomlin caught up as Grandfather reached a chain, thick-as-your-leg, that stretched into the water.

'Stand back!'

Grandfather swung the hammer. Sparks burst as the head struck the narrow end of the wedge, freeing the wedge, hurtling it among the potatoes, and the chain-end escaped down the shore and vanished as if sucked in by the water. The island tilted.

'Hurry, Grandfather!'

Tomlin stared at the wall of fire. Smoke devoured the monument. Smoke poured upwards, hiding the town and the summer sky. A shadow lay over the island as the sun died.

'Get everyone inside!' yelled Grandfather.

Grandfather struck at another wedge and another chain-end slithered away. 'And shut the windows!'

Tomlin fled, shouting; bustling them inside, lifting Sequence. Coughing. All the children weeping. Pick's pea-eye, dry; finding a window in Tomlin's caravan, to gape out at the fire.

The island rocked and moaned. The town roared. Fires exploded in advance of the wall of flame as sparks lit weeds. 'The bees!' gasped Tomlin.

He raced.

He glimpsed Grandfather, and metal banged on metal.

He ran to the bridge. The lawn around the hives smouldered. Bees flew in panic.

'Get away!' gasped Tomlin. 'Get away, bees!' But smoke spread over the lawn towards the bridge.

The island lurched. Grandfather lunged with the

great hammer. 'If y'can't stay inside,' he bellowed, 'rescue the fishing rods! Two chains to go!' And Tomlin ran as he had never run, eyes wet, coughing, between the onions and carrots; above him, the pulley rope flexing like a long thin animal in terror; through the orchard, where a spark burned a hole in a plum tree leaf; down the long slope of potatoes. Above the roar of the town, Tomlin heard the hammer strike. Grandfather had waited for him to reach the rods. If the rods were lost now – ! He snatched them from their clefts in the shore, throwing them on to the grass or into the potatoes.

'Clear!' he screamed.

And the final sharp ring of metal reached him; and the island danced; and the beach beneath the smoke moved upstream. Another metallic noise reached Tomlin, and he knew the bridge had clanged on to its wheels and the wheels had turned as the island slid from under them.

The smoke was less. The shore receded. Tomlin moved through the potatoes trying to stay close to the town.

Grandfather, sweating-wet, stood with him.

They watched the town burn. Smoke formed clouds like clouds full of summer rain. A building fell. Dust and flame leapt, then the sound crashed across the water. Tomlin held Grandfather's hand. He thought of the Poor Souls. They would die soon in the fire. He thought of Bolliter, and wondered if he would see her again as the island pursued her floating carcass.

He wondered at the untold stories; about his mother and father; the sunken yacht; what Grandfather meant by saying he should have existed sooner. He remembered suddenly, Grandfather beating a hole in the wall of Bolliter's kitchen with a single blow.

Tomlin held Grandfather's knuckles to examine them. Blood crusted dark on the skin. He saw Grandfather running ahead along the shore road, running at such speed . . .

Grandfather sighed.

'Grandfather.'

'Mmm.' Grandfather sighed again. 'No more birds,' he murmured. 'Not the blackbird. And the mouse we saw. Remember! Wiped out! Wiped out a second time. For the same reason. For mad fear.'

'Grandfather, how can you run so fast?'

Grandfather, it seemed to Tomlin, stood very still.

'I'll never be as strong as you, Grandfather.'

Sequence came and sat at Grandfather's feet, leaning against his leg. The children, and Pick with Rem, descended the veranda steps. Azalea petals, loosened by the wind rocked on the grass as the island drifted with the current.

'D'you know,' said Grandfather, 'what a metabolic android is?'

'No – '

'No. I'm sure you don't. Just another late twentieth-century experiment. Very successful, it was.'

Grandfather grinned down at Tomlin, then laughed with all his teeth. 'Things to do!' he bellowed.

'But – '

'Time later for stories! D'you know where we're going? D'you know where we're going!' he roared at the children.

The green islands of the Plant sat in the glittering water. The sun rose above the curtain of smoke.

Tomlin pointed. The seagull wheeled over the scattered fishing rods.

'The future,' said Grandfather. He gathered the children around him. He smiled at Pick and Rem. 'Into the future. That's where we're going. Are we up to it? Mm? Can we cope with such a challenge? Well? There's no one else! THERE'S NO ONE ELSE!'

He sighed a great sigh. 'There's no one else,' he whispered.